The Mayisna's War

Book 4: Kialor

By Tiona Yates

Chapter 1

Kialor swung down from his mount almost as soon as they'd reached the group. He had no knowledge of who the person in grey was, or the old man in travel-stained robes, but he did know that his father was here, and that made his heart much lighter. That his cousin Rhiann was also here made a difference too. It was a possible solution to the worries that Maskar had had about trying to hook the gods into the kee-ali-dahlri nature. With a light heart, Kialor almost bounded into an embrace with his father, Ranor, and later took a turn at a hug from Rhiann. Nothing else mattered at the moment, not the two other people, surely.

Even as he regained his bearings after the almost crushing hugs from his elders, he could hear Maskar urge Rhiann to mount up. That made sense. Rhiann shouldn't be walking so far, and Maskar would certainly give up his horse so that his uncle could get the rest needed for his foot. It doubtless was why they'd traveled so slowly. With a false foot, Rhiann would have to go more slowly and take many more breaks.

"I'm alright, Maskar. I was told that someone would almost certainly see us on our way. And it was determined that it was better that we come this way, rather than use other possible transport. They didn't have horses at the scholars' redoubt, so this was on foot, but Ranor, at least, insisted that I rest often and carry less." The Ollahmic priest laughed, eyes twinkling brightly. "I think I should stand, at least, until you have had a chance to see who else is here."

Kialor glanced at the other two figures, noting that the one in grey was merely covered in a heavy over-robe, with the cowl pulled up to disguise their face. After a moment, he decided that they were probably a woman, built too slightly to be a man, unless they were like Maskar himself and quite gaunt. The other was an older man who Maskar winced at the presence of. So, someone his cousin knew, even if he didn't like him. Kialor had to wonder at that, since it seemed unlikely that Maskar would know anyone here.

"Dastyl," the name was almost spat out, "And why are you here?"

The old man smiled, though it wasn't the nicest of smiles, "Maskar, I told you before that there were those of us who opposed the Great Mother and studied different ways. Is it so unlikely that I am here to offer what aid I can to your venture? As well, there is someone who had reason to be cautious, though she's warmed quite nicely to Master Rhiann and Master Ranor."

Kialor turned his attention to the woman in grey since she'd just been confirmed a woman. He saw long-fingered hands emerge from the enveloping sleeves of the robe and move up to the cowl, pulling it back hesitantly. What Kialor saw was astounding, though he understood why within an instant. The hair revealed was like liquid gold through most of it, until the ends, which were almost as red as flame. Eyes were bright green, not uncommon in his family, certainly. The face, well, he didn't have to take more than a moment to realize the truth about it. Even without the scars that he was so familiar with, it was very close to Vishti's, so likely a sister, an older one, it would seem. Another of Redel's get, doubtless.

Dastyl executed a half-bow. "May I present Sai'velk, who, according to the august personage who brought Masters Ranor and Rhiann, is the final person needed for what must be. She was quite taken aback by his presence, doubtless because she realized his blood, even if he had to explain to her her own."

"August personage?" Kialor found that he could manage those words, even if he couldn't manage much more, still staring at the spectacle of Sai'velk.

"I was brought to see the son of my Lord and Master Ranor's Lady," Sai'velk almost purred. "It was difficult at first, even though he said that I hold the blood of my Lord's line and that these two were cousins who would help me in what must be. He said, if we do what is intended, it will be a great victory to the Phoenix, a rebirth of the world in a real way, much as was said to have been done before I was born, when the Earthmother had to be restored."

The Phoenix? Is she saying that she's a priestess of the Risen One? And clearly kee-ali-dahlri, for no human could look quite like that! Kialor was more astounded, realizing that the colors in Sai'velk's appearance were doubtless chosen manifestations of a faith that was largely unheard of by the people here.

Redel seemed hesitant, even as he swung off his horse, studying the woman in front of him, almost like he was studying a vision that didn't really exist. "You call my cousins yours. Is it true as it seems? Another daughter of mine?"

Sihan'el took a deep breath from where he still sat on his horse. "I think I remember her, but from when I was very young. I'm not sure about the name, even though her existence was known. I had no idea where she was or even if she'd escaped. There was vague news that she might have left the Sisterhood before the Mad One turned against us."

Sai'velk nodded, stepping forward, "I would not be able to make a mistake on this, Father." Her use of the word was not nearly as hesitant as either Vishti's or Sihan'el's. "I see you in those the Lord of Gifts brought as my cousins, and I see my echo in the woman's face," she pointed to Vishti. "This means that what was spoken must be true, and I will perhaps find peace and wholeness in the life ahead."

Redel seemed almost afraid to step forward, but he did, spreading his arms, "I hope you are not among those harmed by my choices, Daughter. I would like to think that at least someone of my get was free of the pain of my actions."

She moved gracefully over, well within reach of that hug. Kialor realized that this was perhaps the one opportunity Redel would have to not have pain with such a homecoming. When he saw Redel's arms close around her, he nodded, a smile on his face. This was what Father needed most, someone who openly accepted him, without any hesitation on their part. It was a long moment before any of them moved. When they did, it was because of a faint groan from Rhiann.

Maskar immediately moved to stabilize his uncle, then gestured to the horse. "We don't have a saddle, which might make this harder."

Ranor moved over to where Maskar and Rhiann stood, "Let me help him up. I'm certainly big enough to do that. He does need the rest, and riding should do that. Rhiann, be prepared, as this might be a little faster than you expect." With a heave, Ranor got Rhiann almost thrown up onto the back of the horse, then took a moment to help adjust his cousin's seat so that it would be reasonably easy.

Kialor moved over to where Redel and Sai'velk stood, inclining his head, "My greetings, Cousin, or Sister, depending on how you wish to be called. I married Vishti, though I am yet trying to get the knowledge I need of her. And she is clearly your sister. Perhaps, though, we should get you all to the camp for now. I can take Vishti on my horse, and perhaps you should ride the one she rode in on?"

Sai'velk eyed the horse, then trembled, "I don't think I've ever ridden, so doubt I could handle one, especially without a saddle."

Ranor spoke up, "Mistress Sai'velk, I can mount up, then pull you on to sit before me. You won't fall, and there would be no danger at all. I've been riding since I was a toddler, and there's little chance of me letting anyone fall."

Kialor nodded, "Father had a Steppelander for a mother, and a grandmother, and spent much time around Uncle Kelu, who also came from the Steppe. He probably hasn't fallen since he was five or so. You won't find a better person to keep you on the back of the beast, I think."

He heard Hela call out to Sihan'el, "Since we'll need to get the last person on horseback, lover, you should ride with me. I'm sure you can manage that much. Leave the scholar to your beast, for now."

Kialor moved to mount up, carefully pulling Vishti up behind him, for she would be better able to handle trouble, should it come, if she could slide off herself. He would do better on horseback if trouble came. Even as the arrangements were made, Maskar riding with Evanira, and Redel mounting back up on his charger, Kialor could hear Vishti murmur softly in his ear, "She looks not unlike how I could have been. If I had not been taken by the Sisters for punishment."

Kialor reached back and squeezed her knee, "Vishti, while she is beautiful, there are things about you which are moreso. She is primarily beautiful because she shows a purpose, a faith, something that defines her. You have shown that same sort of total trust with me, and I'm not disappointed with which Calasti sister I ended up with. Do not take my astonishment at her appearance as desire for anything other than what I have. I wouldn't trade you for her, not for any reason. I promised that I wouldn't abandon you, and I'm holding true to that promise."

She shivered, putting her arms around his waist, just where they reminded his body of her presence. "You didn't want me, not at first. Yet you seem so certain now?"

He held his breath a moment, then whispered back to her, "Vishti, you saw what I did not, at first. I wasn't ready to see the truth, though I've seen it since. If you need proof of this, you need only recognize that it was your touch, not her appearance, that caused that reaction a moment ago. I won't leave you, and I wouldn't even consider anyone else, not now that I've seen what you do to me. It's been uncomfortable at times, but sometimes I need discomfort, just to remind me of the life I need to live."

He was tempted to say something beyond the words he had already spoken but felt it wasn't right. He just wasn't ready to speak out certain words. His heart wasn't entirely decided on them yet.

Chapter 2

Sihan'el worked with Hela to rub down the horses after they returned, though he really wanted to find out more about the sister he only vaguely remembered. She seemed so serene, so peaceful, and he found that very hard to believe in a woman who was older than he was and raised very strongly among the kril'dga. He couldn't remember who her mother was said to be, but there was something about that poise, that natural calm, that transcended his understanding. Vishti might be calm usually due to what had been done to her mind to protect her. But that wasn't the sense that Sihan'el got from Sai'velk. Nor was there any pretense to her taking the term for claw. It was clear that she wanted little to do with the claws at all.

Hela murmured to him from where she stood, noting that Ranor was also helping out with the horses. Doubtless, Rhiann would have too, except he'd been ushered to a place where he could sit. Which might be challenging enough, since Sihan'el was vaguely aware of the fact that the Ollahmic priest had a false foot, and might find it difficult to get up and down much. "We'll get a chance to talk to her, lover, but I think it's best to let her father get started with that. Trust me, he's almost breaking inside with what he is feeling. And considering the good turn he did us a few days ago, giving me the knowledge to make things much easier, well, I don't think you can complain too much at him getting the first chance to find out what's in her heart, can you?"

He looked down, not wanting to speak up on that, especially with another close relative at hand, "I just want to be a part of things, I guess, Hela. And I'm still unsure of what happened two nights ago, well, other than the obvious. I don't understand why you would act as you did, why you weren't angry with me when you should have been. It doesn't make any sense to me. Finding out about my sister might be easier to handle."

She glanced over at Ranor, made some sort of sign that Sihan'el couldn't read, then stopped what she was doing and walked directly at Sihan'el. A moment later, he found her mouth on his, no way to hide what he was doing, only accept that that was what she wanted. Certainly, it was pleasant, but it made him feel far more awkward and confused since nothing had made sense since she'd allowed him control. He still could hardly believe that she wanted his touch and wasn't making him pay for seeing her at her weakest. All he knew was that he didn't want her angry with him, not now or ever.

When she'd gotten done with that, she smiled and tilted her head at him, "Sihan'el, I admit that I was surprised at how wrong I was about your father. He showed a different type of vulnerability to me when he explained what he'd been through. I'm willing to explain that if you want, but he'd be better at doing it since you'd have less fear of lies from him, at least if you understand what that sword of his really means. I don't think you need to worry about Ranor, though. I know enough of him to know that he'll keep his peace. If only because he doesn't want other things brought up."

There was a snort from the other side of the corral. "Aunt, I'm going to keep my peace not because of that, but simply because there's no way I'm going to get in the middle of an argument between you and Grandfather. Either of them. I don't need to know anything more than that you've clearly been making offerings to my Goddess. I know my son enough to know that, even if Redel hasn't insisted on precautions, Kialor would have. I know his herb lore is decent in that area, so you're going to be kept on that at the moment."

Sihan'el shivered, moving to work on the next horse. But he did risk speaking to the green-garbed priest as he worked with a will on those beasts. "I don't understand anyone. Kialor might not have approved, but it seems that no one else is saying a single thing against this, though I've been given the impression that it would be frowned upon where you come from."

"The only frowning upon it that would be done there would be concern for any children that might come," Ranor replied, checking the horse's hooves carefully and digging out a knife to trim that back just right. "Honestly, you might offer a chance to someone else, depending on what comes of my aunt's current fascination with you. You don't know Maskar's son Brehl, or Rhiann's daughter Yossa. Neither has looked anywhere else for companionship and if things work out between you and Hela, well, it might be considered that a bond between Yossa and Brehl might not be entirely negative. I've already considered it, brought it before my Goddess. She's given me a reason to wait and see, for now. I think you might be a good reason why that might be."

Sihan'el looked up, startled, then saw Hela look away quickly. She'd been watching him during that conversation, and something had her disturbed, at least a little bit. Then he caught sight of a faint coloring of her fair skin. That didn't make much of any sense to him, much like nothing else had made sense in almost a tenday now. "What is it that the two of you are meaning? I don't understand any of it, not at all."

Ranor laughed, "By the Goddess, you don't see it, do you? I'm not sure I should speak what's been obvious almost from the time she pulled you up onto the back of her horse. And that's something she really doesn't do. Aunt Hela is very particular about her stallion. I understand why, too. Especially pulling a man up onto it behind her."

Sihan'el blinked, looking back and forth between the two. "I don't understand. We just needed to get back here, didn't we?"

Ranor coughed, "Aunt, it seems that you're going to have to take him aside for a talk, at least before you make your intentions any more clear to the rest of us. I knew what I saw on both sides, but I have personal experience with both types of situations. You know that, aside from high respect for her place and appreciation for her beauty, I had no feelings at all for Laira, though I feel strongly enough about Lyris. From something Uncle Telin had said, I had guessed that there was a game in play. I arrive here and find that it's not a game at all. Or not anymore."

Hela shrugged and glanced back over at where Ranor and Sihan'el were standing. "Ranor, your son pointed out that sometimes, truth needs to be the basis for things. And I learned a lot from an experiment of sorts, things I wasn't ready to deal with. So, yes, things are changing. I really haven't had the opportunity to let him see those changes or point out that they seem to have changed on both sides."

Ranor nodded, and Sihan'el tried to understand what was being said, "You mentioned that this is not a game, a trading of power, anymore? I do not understand, not really."

Ranor shook his head, "Cousin, I want you to think, just for a moment. Something changed the rules you were working by, just a few days ago, didn't they?"

"I know that I grew frustrated at things, and she offered me something I could not refuse, but, in accepting, I did things I know I should not have done. Since then, I've been trying to make up for those mistakes, though she hasn't acted, at least these past days, like they were mistakes. I don't understand. Any woman here would have been close to gutting me for seeing them at such weakness. Yet she, who serves a master of destruction, does not."

Ranor looked at Hela with narrowed eyes, then said words in an almost icy voice, "It's now a question of whether you tell him or I do, Aunt. If it's not explained, it will only get worse."

Hela moved over to Sihan'el, face unreadable. Then, with halting words, she spoke, "Your father told me what would change in you while I was still trying to make sense of my own feelings after giving you that power. He told me about your background and what it would do to you. He also didn't forbid anything further but suggested that, if I felt I was ready to take that step, there were things that would make it easier. He saw something I didn't. He saw that we do more than work well together. In letting you experience something new, something that freed you, as it were, from the darkness of your own background, he said that you would be better able to appreciate what could be. He just wasn't as sure about me. He guessed, but wasn't sure. When I came to him, halfway through my cycles, and told him that I thought it a possibility, the change he'd expected, he told me what would help you reach the stage I now knew I wanted."

"And what is it that you do want, Hela?"

"I want to find something I long had feared, a position where I'm working, give and take, with someone who's just as capable as I am, and yet, who also wants my happiness. No one else has dared to do as much as you did, and it made me realize that I want more than mere pleasure for as long as this war continues."

Sihan'el felt almost as if his world had shifted suddenly. He was seeing her again, the way he'd demeaned her to an extent that night, the way she'd been almost begging him to finish things. He saw her at her most vulnerable, and, while there was still a sense of wanting power, he also found that it was accompanied by a desire to keep her at his side. Indeed, he acknowledged within himself that he was terrified of ever having to look for someone else. And now, if he was reading her right, she was offering some form of permanence.

Ranor shrugged, "Theoretically, before we've finished what we're here to do, I could make this quite safe for the two of you. I do serve Jirel, even if you both seem to have forgotten that. A bond of the earth, that's within my capabilities."

Sihan'el swallowed hard, looking at Hela, still shaking from the change. Hela merely smiled, patted his face, then glanced over at Ranor. "I think he needs to recover before he can decide." There was no question of her decision. She was waiting on his.

Chapter 3

Vishti felt restless, especially after seeing a woman that there was little doubt was her sister. Sai'velk was beautiful, beautiful as she could have been if things hadn't been different. And Sai'velk seemed at peace, as if there was little in the world that could destroy that peace as if there was little that could affect her deeply. She had accepted a hug from Father almost immediately and had carried herself almost like she was a princess born, which seemed strange, as the Sisters, at least, were ranked on their seniority, and Sai'velk would have left the kril'dga at a fairly early age, at least if what was said made any sense. There was a hint that she'd left before the issues with the Mad One, but had not yet elaborated on that issue. Mostly, she was quiet, almost like a ghost given form.

It was only when Kialor moved to take Vishti's hand in his that she realized that her husband was still very much at her side. His eyes might be resting on Sai'velk, but he had promised, and she knew he meant his promises, that he would not leave her, not for any reason. That was something that she needed to know. She needed to have faith in him because her faith elsewhere was shaky at best. Having seen her mother, and the fact that her brother had known for so long, those had shaken her understanding of the world. She wasn't sure what was real anymore. She needed some form of that reality to be brought to her.

"Vishti," Kialor hissed at her, "you should go to greet your sister. She is almost certainly not at fault for what happened to you, if you think about it. She's family, and I imagine she wants to know her family, at least if what I'm reading from her is to be known. I don't think she dislikes you. But you need to get over your own dislike of her."

"Why do you think I dislike her?" Vishti knew her statement was too rushed, pitched just wrong enough that Kialor would know the truth.

He turned and pulled her to him, kissing her cheeks and then her lips, "Because I have enough female relatives that I know when a woman gets a touch jealous. And you are more than a touch so. There's no reason to be, Vishti. Nothing has made you any less than you were this morning. Nothing has made my dedication to be at your side any less. Just as you accepted your father on my behalf and even went to meet his wife and your other sisters and brother, you can do this, for me, if for no other reason. I think that she's possibly even a bit afraid of you. She certainly will be able to see what I do, your fear, and your anger. Let's not let that anger fester any longer. You'll know that she can be trusted if you take the time to find out. That's all I'm asking of you."

She looked at him, saw the hint of pain in his expression, and that was one thing she wanted to wipe out, even if it meant making peace with someone who had what she could not, the peace of growing up without pain, without the memory of fear and humiliation. "Then I will go. I know to listen to you, even if it is not entirely what I want."

He led her through the camp to a place where Rhiann was perched awkwardly on a short barrel, the closest thing they seemed to have for a proper chair. His leg dangled slightly, but it was likely more comfortable, considering his foot. There was Father, speaking softly to Sai'velk, a wry smile on his face. It was a look he'd used with Vishti before, and, if she remembered aright, La'halsi. Vishti pulled herself to her full height, her head held high, and squared her shoulders to approach where Father and Sai'velk and Rhiann were talking. Kialor didn't seem to feel the need to look so proud, but he didn't stray more than a step away from her as she moved. He was at least keeping that much of his promise.

Father glanced over, and a slightly brighter smile came on his face. He extended a hand in her direction and nodded to Kialor, "And now, perhaps, we'll have more of the family. Sai'velk, you said you hadn't had a chance to meet Vishti before?"

The golden-haired woman shook her head, inclining her head toward Vishti. "I knew that there were others, though I'd only met Sihan'el, once, while he was small. I was several years older and always felt a little strange. I recognized him when I saw him, though his face had changed. That is the result of becoming an adult, I think. I left too early to get to know any of the rest of my family. And my mother was not inclined to share what she had, either her power or her possessions, and I seemed to be well considered one of the latter."

Father moved to grasp Vishti, to hug her, just as he'd hugged Sai'velk. "Vishti, I was just learning some things of great import. I haven't had a chance to learn much other than that Lord Mikedel, son of the Risen One and Jirel, was the one to bring our family here, or rather, to a place of safety and learning nearby. It is well sealed, which is why they haven't had much trouble with the constructs yet. It's likely where we'll be performing our Music. Someplace where the enemies would have a harder time reaching us."

He brushed his lips against her forehead. "We're still going to need you, Vishti. Sai'velk has another purpose, and I've already figured that out. She is the only one of our people who serves the Risen One. We'll have representatives of the entire council, one way or another. You're still going to have to power it, though it will be easier on Maskar, if nothing else, to have someone else he can work with to steady the protections so that we can do what we need to do."

Vishti pulled away gently, unsure how her father could be so quick to accept. "Kialor said that I should come to know my sister. I'm not sure what I am to know other than that she bears your blood, Father."

Sai'velk moved over to her, inclining her head. "Sister, there is much that you can learn, much that might make you what you are yet afraid of. You are one that everyone hopes for because you can do what the rest of us cannot. You have pain, and I can understand. Just because you do not see the marks of what I've been through does not mean that I do not understand your anger right now. You have that anger because you do not know the truth, what happened."

Kialor inclined his head, "Then, Sister, could you tell us these things? It might make it easier on her since the focus of her pain has become all too obvious to her in recent days."

Sai'velk gestured to a place by the fire. "Then sit, and I will tell you how I came to leave the Sisterhood, how I cast the title of claw from my name and found an answer that I did not expect."

As the others sat, Sai'velk knelt down on the rocky ground, closing her eyes for a long moment before speaking. There was a sense about her that Vishti was wary of, some sense of purpose that was beyond mortal understanding. "I knew, early, that my mother intended me for a weapon. I had strength of purpose and knowledge of many things, but I was never allowed to choose anything for myself. I was dominated, even after I had come into my own power. Any deviation from what my mother wanted was punished, and that was a lesson I learned early. She did not mark me, but used other means to ensure that I dared not disobey. I found that was too much to bear, and, though I have since found out that there is a resistance, a group who disobeyed the orders they were given, I was not approached by them. It was too much of a risk, I believe. Instead, I used the knowledge I'd been given to find secret ways out of Methil'dga. I left without a word, and without leaving the message I had wanted to, a dagger buried in my mother's chest. Since then, I have been told that that was perhaps the thing that made what happened later possible. I did not strike out in vengeance, though I had wanted it. That purity, even when caused by fear of what might happen to me if I did strike out, was what allowed the Phoenix to send his servant to me.

"I took only what I needed and carefully traveled south through the mountains. There was still danger. There were still patrols among the people of the south that sought to cage others. Because of my beauty, because of the power that I had, I was desirable, and I was taken, convinced to drink something laced with drugs, and awoke in chains. If there was more done to me, I am not aware, only aware of the chains that bound me and the insults thrown at me while I was marched further south."

"So, captives of the Toyurasan, that is not a good thing, though I know they had to change some of that." Redel's voice was soft, pained to an extent.

"I was saved by another who had felt the sting of the whip from those golden-skinned fiends. He came out of nowhere, killing the slavers who had taken many of those they could find in the mountains. They called him something, a golden ghost, and tried to use some of us to stay his hand. I do not know how it was, but I could feel as if I were burning from within, even as the slaver took his blade to set against my chin. Moments later, he was screaming, backing off in shock. I realized that I was encased in fire, fire that did not burn me. That was enough to frighten the slavers, and they fled and were picked off by that golden ghost. Then he returned with a key to remove my bonds and the bonds of everyone still chained. He bowed to me, and said that the Phoenix had to have a purpose for me."

Redel looked at Rhiann, who nodded, "Doubtless Xereff, and likely only a few years after Maskar and Virea did their Great Music. I'm almost surprised he never mentioned her in Sharlan. Maybe he didn't understand, then, what she meant, why she could do what no others of the People could. And perhaps he'd forgotten the facts he learned by the time he came to know you."

"Yes, the golden ghost goes by the name of Xereff. He spent many days walking with me, teaching me of his belief, of his certainty that the Phoenix meant for me to do something. He gave me a medallion, one he had carved himself, and taught me the first of my prayers. He told me that revenge was not something he served and that the Phoenix would bring such healing as I needed. In the end, he and I found the place of scholars, hidden deep within the mountain. He knew one of them, Dastyl, but said little of his experiences. He left me there, saying that, though he was awed by the way I took to the Phoenix' worship, there was someone else in his heart. I wonder after that, that he could choose where most in Methil'dga cannot. But he merely said that I would come to understand in time. He left many years ago, and I haven't seen him since."

Vishti listened, but her heart was not moved toward Sai'velk, not yet. She only knew that this woman seemed to have a surety that she did not have and power that she would never have. The anger might have grown less with the story, but not enough to stop it. That might change in time if Kialor was right, but it would take time.

Chapter 4

"So you were rather shocked into silence when Lord Mikedel showed up with my nephew and cousin? I find that slightly amusing. Especially the idea that you immediately fell to your knees before him when he appeared. Sai'velk, you are kin to him as well, though that might not have been explained to you. Lord Mikedel is half-brother to Lady Mialar, our distant grandmother. We have the blood of both brother gods in us." Hela took a few minutes to try to ease some of the nervousness that the kee-ali-dahlri woman might have with Hela's intentions to snare Sihan'el as a permanent partner, though he'd said nothing more on the issue, seeming to need plenty of time to himself for now. She figured she'd let that go for a few days, enough time for Rhiann to recover from his walk, and then they'd work on getting to the sanctuary mentioned that Dastyl was from.

"Why should I not find myself in shock and awe at the presence of my Lord's own son? While the others seem familiar with him, I cannot imagine that any priest would be immune to such awe when they first met them."

Hela chuckled, "I wasn't there for Ranor's first meeting with Mikedel, and he hadn't dedicated himself to Jirel yet, but I can say that his reaction was less awe and more shock at what was revealed there. It took a few days before the rest of us were informed, but I'd say that if you're so shocked at Mikedel, you shouldn't be so comfortable with my nephew. Mikedel is Ranor's maternal grandfather. His mother, the Steppelander Hlasa, was Mikedel's own daughter, though that wasn't found out until his brother was an adult, and Ranor himself was nearing that. He can probably tell you a little more about the situation, but I imagine that he'll firstly try to remind you that even the demi-divine have chosen bonds with the mortal world. I believe that may always be the case, though it took Mikedel the longest to do so."

Sai'velk stared at her, her hand rising to cover a mouth that had fallen open. "You are certain? Mikedel has children?"

"A single child, now long dead. I think Mikedel regretted that he could do so little for Hlasa, who was intended as a mercy to a woman who would have died had she not borne a child and whose mate was incapable of providing her such. The Lord of Gifts did gift each of his grandsons weapons that suited them, weapons of heavenly make. Beyond that, well, he shows up from time to time. Usually on his divine parents' business, but occasionally for other reasons. I gather that he tried to hide himself from view during Hlasa's funeral, but those there who knew the truth, which was pretty much only the family, as Hlasa didn't like outside contact, recognized his presence. I'd say that he loved her well, if from afar."

Sai'velk shivered, looking distinctly uncomfortable, "How could either of the two, being priests, be able to reconcile their devotion to such casual contact with the divine?"

Hela smiled, "I've come in contact with the purely mortal son of my Lord regularly. After a time, you get used to that. Lord Vythen favors his son, Zenir, but he does not insist on any position or power being given to him. Zenir is an uncle in two ways, for me. He married my Aunt Rinah, and he's a distant uncle because his half-brother Daevor was one of the founders of our line. I can also say that, while Ranor hasn't met any of the actual gods himself yet, only the demi-divine, Rhiann ended up with a number of shocks that we're lucky he survived, the day he met his god. It would take him a few moons before he decided that he really had no choice but to take up the vocation he'd been denying for years. You might want to talk to him about it sometime. Most people end up on their knees when facing the divine, as Grandfather Arandel did. Rhiann, however, had no choice on how he met his Lord. He was sprawled out on the floor of a room in a ruin, blood pooling around the leg that had just lost its foot. And that was the time when Rhiann found out the truth, that the daughter he'd adopted some fifteen years before was actually the blood-daughter of Lord Ollahm. That might have been a humbling experience, but I don't think Rhiann's ever needed humbling. It's never been in his nature to take too much pride in anything."

This was apparently too much for Sai'velk, who seemed to collapse, her hands over her face. Hela hadn't intended to shock the woman quite that much, but it was clear that the idea of such casual interactions with the divine was too much for the priestess. It was something she likely would have to learn the better of, soon, because the family was often favored with direct contact, though Grandfather Arandel had always said that his contact with Railah had always been either after he'd just made a huge mistake or just before he would make one.

The fall of the phoenix priestess alerted some of those around that there was trouble. Almost surprisingly, Rhiann was the first to arrive, hobbling over at what amounted to almost a run for him. "What is wrong? I know you were talking, but this? Did you speak ill of her father, perhaps?"

Hela shook her head, "No, I just informed her of truths that seem to have overcome her. I didn't realize that she would be unable to understand those, Cousin."

He bent down, reaching for Sai'velk's hand, "Please, Cousin, stand up. You seem to have taken a bit of a shock, though I'm sure that Hela had not intended it. She might be a little reckless, but that is not surprising, considering her own vocation. Lord Vythen is known to value quick action, perhaps a bit too much. Though he seemed more considerate when I encountered him. He gave his son words that no one expected, and, well, he seemed to understand my own depth of pain at the time."

Sai'velk's voice was faint as she tried to speak, "You encountered one of the brother gods? In person?"

Rhiann pulled her to her feet, not an easy trick with his balance. "Cousin, at the time, I was really in no condition to appreciate the honor of his embrace, though I understand it now and find it one of the greatest things I have experienced. I in no way deserved that honor, but I have been told that he has a gentle side, perhaps not even all of his followers know. But if contact with the divine leaves you so weak, I would say you need to listen to those who know best. Maskar has had contact with both my daughter Nefta, who is also Lord Ollahm's daughter, and with Lord Vythen himself, who came when Maskar's son and my daughter were taken. There was much involved with that theft of our kin. It was not lightly that the gods interfered, though Vythen's son's mother, Iltres, is mother to my younger daughter, the one who was taken. No, they interfered because the nature of the attack was one that they needed answers to. It was the start of what we believe is now the root of our troubles. The Great Mother would not have acquired the weapons she had, had not the borders between Rigedh and this world been erased."

Sai'velk shuddered, and Rhiann put an arm around her, then glanced at Hela, "So you were explaining our connections to the gods. I am not surprised, though I wish you had been more cautious. She has none of our understanding, Cousin, our background. We grew up with this. She did not. Just finding her father may be enough to shock her. Finding out about the rest of our family? That would be distressing indeed."

Hela nodded, feeling the rebuke though it was not said with anything more than a gentle tone of worry toward Sai'velk. Rhiann never did have to raise his voice or even use any type of anger or scorn. It just wasn't his way. A few words, gentle enough, would convince anyone of their errors. She didn't know how he did it, but he always had.

"I didn't realize, considering that she really can't have been a priestess for that long, that she would have such a feeling of awe regarding the gods and their children."

"I know that you intended well, Cousin, but perhaps a little more thought before you speak might prevent this from happening again. Now, Sai'velk, perhaps it would be best if we went to find a place for us to lay out our own bedrolls. It will be difficult for me to rise in the morning, but not impossible. If I ask for help, know that it is not requesting anything but aid in moving, because my leg does not work well at bringing me up from the ground. Hela will likely have her own problems to sort out soon enough, and I should hope that she takes a little more care with those, for I will be less able to aid in resolving that." If there was a rebuke in that at all, it was the warning that Hela would have to take greater care in dealing with Sihan'el. Indeed, she wasn't sure that he would want her sleeping near him, not tonight, while he coped with the realizations that had been revealed today.

"Cousin," Hela decided to speak helpfully, "I recall that there's room near where Maskar and Evanira sleep. If anyone would be willing to help you, no matter the difficulty, it would be Maskar. I don't think he'd even consider it any kind of a burden. You saw how eager he was to offer you his horse. Of all of us, I think you've had the most impression on him."

Rhiann chuckled, "It seems that way, certainly. And I think that might be the best idea. It would be safer, not only for me, but for Sai'velk, who has not been away from her sanctuary for many years now. Maskar is perhaps better protection than most, and with Evanira, well, I doubt anything would get close enough to cause problems."

Hela nodded, letting Rhiann lead off Sai'velk, then decided she wouldn't risk forcing Sihan'el to decide anything just yet. He needed time, and she'd give it. She moved to collect her own bedroll. Perhaps she'd do best alone for tonight. She just didn't want that to last.

Chapter 5

Kialor suggested that Vishti go and practice for now, knowing that she'd worry too much if he left her without giving a reason. She'd been more than needy the prior night, almost clinging to him. He knew that he'd have to find some solution to her fears regarding her sister, but he didn't have the answer. However, he was fairly certain he knew who might. Of all of the people here, he knew that his father might have the most insight into a woman's jealousy. It had been Mother's jealousy of Laira, in the rite that had created Lyris, that had made their relationship work. It had only worked, though, because Ranor had made it clear that he'd had no attachment at all to Laira. Kialor needed to know the best way to make that clear to Vishti before things got far worse.

"Father," Kialor cleared his throat, seeing a flash of Jirellian green ahead of him. It wasn't robes; Father rarely wore those, but it was Jirellian green, standard for any priest or priestess of the Earthmother. He hadn't seen who his father was talking to and was immediately at least a little embarrassed to find that the term applied to another, as well, right there.

The two older men laughed as they realized they were both responding to him, then Redel gestured him closer. "I've grown so used to you calling me that that it took me a moment to realize that you might mean Ranor. Come on over. You weren't interrupting anything important."

Kialor inclined his head to both of them. "It might be a good thing that I have you both because, though it might be less something you can do," he gestured to Redel, "you may still have to deal with the aftereffects, and well, they might be troublesome if I don't find a solution."

Ranor chuckled, "Something that serious, is it, son? And let me guess: it concerns that beautiful redhead of yours?"

"If only she realized how beautiful she still is, or that those marks on her aren't anything to be ashamed of, but signs of how much she's fought past, how much she's overcome over the years. She can't help but see something different when she looks at her sister, and she does not realize that Sai'velk means her no ill. She hardly remembers that I intend to keep my promise, never abandon her, and care for her as entirely as I can."

Ranor seemed unable to help the laugh, "The one woman who's managed to get you out of your comfort zone, and she's still not satisfied with that? She's had far more than anyone could have convinced you of before. Or at least, I'm assuming that's the case. I would think that your requesting those potions meant that there was more done than perhaps merely holding her."

Kialor looked down, "She's had more than just being held many times since we left and that one night before. I can even say that I've not even been particularly resistant to that because, while it took a while to get used to her, I've found that I am more whole with her in my arms. I just don't know how to explain it to her in a way she'll understand. Or a way to help her lose the anger and jealousy she has regarding her sister. I'm not sure how she feels about the others anymore, either. She hadn't gotten to the point of knowing she had what she wanted when we left Sharlan. She might end up just as jealous of Ma'enda and La'halsi."

Redel sighed from where he stood, hands folded across his chest. In that, despite the sword-hilts showing behind his right shoulder, he looked a lot like his father, Uncle Jalak. There was that same sense of total solidity in his presence, like he couldn't be moved by force, and yet, very easily, could be moved by something as simple as love. It was an odd dichotomy that they both had. It might have been why Vishti warmed so quickly to her father. He was able to channel that sense that he did love her and always would.

"Vishti still has her vanity, though I'm not sure that this is entirely that. From what I'd seen, especially with her frosty attitude toward her sister last night, she still hasn't recovered fully from the shocks at the keep we raided. I wasn't sure before how badly she's hurt, but this makes it more certain. She's caught in a loop of feeling that she's the victim of so much, and, in many ways, she was, but she doesn't have to be, and I'm not sure how to show her the other way. I think she needs to be able to see herself as someone who can handle nearly anything, and I think she can. She just needs to be shown."

Ranor glanced between Kialor and Redel, then nodded quietly. "I do know about jealousy, and in this, she's probably jealous of a lot more than her sister. Sai'velk just happens to be a convenient target at the moment. Redel, you told me about what you'd found out from her mother and her brother. My guess is that there's a much more deeply based jealousy in there, something that won't be easy to uncover and heal. Indeed, it might take another burst of anger to heal that, to make her see what she's doing to herself. I just don't know how you could get her to become angry at the right things, the things that are causing this situation in the first place."

"Father, could you give me any advice?" Kialor was almost desperate for a means to make things a little better, even if all he could do was a little.

"Kialor, the problem is that her jealousy is over many things. Her brother, and now her sister, didn't have to face the tortures she did. She knows her brother had contact with her mother that she lacked and is jealous of that and of the fact that he was allowed to hold a secret that she could not. She's jealous of her sister's beauty, and perhaps her mother's, though I'm less certain. She's probably jealous over Hela's having Sihan'el's total attention right now. In truth, she feels that there's almost nothing that she has of her own, and because of that, she's fighting to keep the only thing she can hold onto hers. She feels like a breath of wind could take away everything. And she doesn't want to share. She won't want to share. It's like being given a broken toy. At least in her current state."

Redel winced, "Which puts me in an entirely untenable situation, considering that I now have three children here, all of whom need my help and deserve my care. I can't favor one over another, even though Vishti needs so much. Right now, it seems that Sihan'el also needs a lot, and I doubt I've even begun to scratch the surface of finding out what Sai'velk needs. I can't give Vishti all of the attention, though that's something she'd want."

Kialor felt his hope of resolving things ebb, like the wax draining away from a candle. "I don't know how to answer her losses or that she does have to share her father's attention. And, at some times, mine. There's so much I have to do, and I can't give her everything she wants. There's not enough time or energy to do that."

Ranor rubbed absently at the sheaf and sickle medallion he wore. "Perhaps that excess of time and effort isn't what she most needs. I imagine that what she needs isn't far off from what Emi needed when she made her choice. Kialor, you've mentioned so far how you care about her, the worries you have over her safety and sanity. But there are other things that perhaps she needs that she's not getting, things that would make a bigger impression. You have to have the pivotal point in this, if only because of your relationship with her. Even if she doesn't understand our ways so much, I'm fairly certain that she knows the concepts of the terms you gave her when you gave her Trade. The question is whether you're willing to admit to something that might make all the difference for her."

Kialor looked up, trying to gauge what his father meant. "I've told her that I won't abandon her, that I'll always be there to care for her."

"But have you expressed your desire for her or the feelings that seem evident in your expression? There are doubtless words you need to say to her. When I was facing the strong possibility of my death, I called your mother vaeh'la, and she was nearly aghast at the fact that I was showing my own feelings at that time, when she thought she'd have to lose me. It gave her the strength to pull off the impossible, find a way to keep me safe. It also almost killed her doing so. You need to tell her those feelings that have remained silent so far. That might give her more of a sense of balance than anything else. I know you probably feel that you aren't ready. The question is whether that need for readiness outweighs her need for peace. And that's something you have to decide, son."

Redel cleared his throat. "Perhaps that should go for me, too. While it would be much more awkward to express that sentiment toward Sihan'el, who's rather lost with his feelings right now anyhow, I could very much go to Vishti and try to tell her how proud I am to be her father, how much I do love her and want her to feel wanted. It might be worth more than the words I've given her so far. I don't know if my words will be as important as Kialor's, but they might be necessary."

Kialor took in a deep breath, "No, Father, I haven't told her that I love her, not yet. I hadn't been certain, though I knew that my feelings were heading in that direction. I just wanted to be able to feel like I'm giving her the truth when I say it. And I don't know yet that it is truth."

Ranor put his hand on Kialor's shoulder, "Son, sometimes you have to say things first, then make them the truth. You have the means to pull that off, even if you don't realize it. You're well on your way to feeling those words, but it will take some time. Repeating them often to her will make it easier. It will make it more the truth each time you say it. And, if you give her the reason to believe in the truth that will be, she'll be stronger and happier. Perhaps, even, her brother should be advised of the same, because that might make the difference in her arguments with him. But she does need to know she's loved. That's the first step to her true healing."

Kialor shivered, then nodded, "Thank you, Father. You gave me advice I needed, even if I don't feel I'm ready for it. I'll go over to catch her attention in a bit. Maybe she'll understand my reluctance if I make it clear that I am here for her and always will be."

"That should do a great deal, son. Now, smile; you have just admitted that you do, in some way, love that beauty of yours. It should take away some of the sting of the situation she put you in. You aren't violating your principles. You just needed time to realize that." Ranor quickly embraced Kialor, then nodded. "You have a fine wife. You just need to understand what she needs better."

Chapter 6

Sihan'el had spent most of the day trying to figure out how to approach the situation between himself and Hela. What she'd indicated was probably not what her family, at least, would prefer in a marriage. It wasn't a statement of love, though his understanding of love was limited at best. It was an offer of a partnership, something permanent. It was more than he thought he deserved, but the indication he'd gotten from Hela was that it was something she wanted, and since it did work in his favor, he realized that he should consider the situation carefully. He really wished he knew more of what Father had told her but wasn't yet bold enough to ask him about that. Especially not if what Hela had used on him was indeed what Father had mentioned that someone had used on him. That was just a little too personal.

Really, he decided, he needed answers from Hela. What she'd told him so far only answered a few of the questions he had. And there was so much more that he needed to know. While he imagined that Father would probably be a good person to have when he finally made his decision, at least to make sure that whatever bargain was sealed was sealed fairly, some things weren't good to discuss publicly. And some of the things he needed to know to come to that decision were in that category.

He found her in the section of camp she'd moved off to last night, probably trying to give him room. He didn't intend to give her any, not this time. If she had liked his taking control when offered, he might just take it more often, try to keep her on her toes. But that depended largely on whether that was what she'd wanted from him.

"Hela, I think there are things that need to be cleared up before we get into a situation that leaves me vulnerable to the dictates of your parents. And that could very well happen, should I let things progress as you seem to want them. Are you willing to talk and promise truth to me? I can't enforce it, not without getting my father into this, but I should hope that, if you want something valuable, you might decide that truth is your best option."

She looked up from where she had been sitting, seemingly deep in thought. "I had wondered when your need for answers would motivate you, lover. Come on and sit. I think that perhaps my nephew was right; at least Kialor was. Truth might just make things work where they would be impossible elsewise."

Sihan'el sat down on the edge of her bedroll, facing her, his hands for the moment resting on his knees. "You sounded, last night, like you were actually far from upset over what I'd done when you'd offered that first bargain. I will take that as truth because it's the only thing that makes what you'd done a few nights back make any sense at all. So, you enjoyed seeing me in that light? You found something that makes you decide you're not going to run off when this war is ended?"

Hela leaned back a moment, leaving his eyes straying down a little too far, to shapes that were hidden under her tunic. That was probably just what she wanted, too, but he couldn't break his gaze away from there for a long moment, remembering the flesh and how it had felt under his hands. "Why should I have been upset at you showing what I've always known was hiding just below the surface? The fact was, though, that you dared what no other had, not one of the lovers I'd taken over the past century or so. You showed me something I wasn't expecting but found that I did enjoy, since you asked that specifically. I don't think I'd ever even vaguely considered that Mother might be right, that a strong man is worth so much more than someone who's worrying too much about pleasing me. When you dropped your pretense of being servant, you immediately became much more interesting, and the excitement you'd seen there was real. It lasted far longer than I'd expected, hence my avoiding you for the first day or so. I'm hoping to get to see more of that, someone who challenges me, rather than merely meekly obeying me."

He listened, trying to put things into place. By the very earth itself, she'd wanted little more than someone who matched her? That was something none of the women here would have accepted. It was likely even true of Vishti. She certainly did not seem to push Kialor to take a stand as anything other than her protector. If there was more that he did, it certainly didn't make itself apparent. But Hela, well, she seemed almost eager for some sign of that challenge.

"And that's why you're actually considering what that priest suggested, a bond of the earth? You think that that challenge won't wear away with time, that you're willing to accept the binding of your freedom? I want to know the truth of that, Hela, before I make any decisions of my own. What you want is important, but, as you'd said, I need to be able to choose this, and it's not going to be a simple decision, as there is far too much to consider still."

"Like that son of yours who may or may not have been killed in an attack, or possibly afterward? I did discuss that with your father, in addition to everything else. His suggestion was perhaps the most practical in this. He suggested that, if I could get your agreement, I would do the same thing Ael'yn promised regarding his offspring. I would offer to stand in as a mother for your son and perhaps any others that might exist that you don't know about, and that is clearly a possibility. As to my reasoning, could you consider that the Dread Lord doesn't like stagnation, and my games were becoming stagnant, he decided? With someone to keep me on my toes and push me to become more than I am, perhaps I'll keep his favor. I doubt I'll succeed any other way. Permanence isn't necessarily stagnation, depending on what it is that is permanent."

"And how do you think I'll push you to the favor of this god you serve? I'm hardly one of his worshippers. I am merely one man who's been fighting for his people's safety."

"*Our* people's safety, Sihan'el. That is very true and will be even more true once Maskar gets us to do this working of his. We are in this together. In more than one way, I suspect. I haven't decided exactly where I might go after this war is won, but perhaps we can start bringing the faith to our people's homeland, Sihan'el. Would that interest you? Bringing me among our own, even if you hardly know them yourself? You would still have more knowledge than I would, because you've spent enough time among the claws and their renegades. You would have a position of power and be encouraged to reach for more. I'm not giving up everything. But I think I liked the way you handled yourself, both with respect for me and with a surge of pride that you've largely hidden since Sharlan. I want to see that pride again, perhaps be the reason."

He sniffed at the air, noting what it told him about the woman sitting across from him. So, she wanted pride and power. He had a possible method, though it might get some trouble elsewhere, to verify what she said in a very real way. And, though he'd held himself back so often before, he knew that he had the strength to pull this off, even if she was just as much of the People as he was, physically. He had too much of his father's build for her to throw off easily. She'd get a chance to deny it, but only by closing herself off completely would she stop this. It was a final test, and it would tell him exactly what he still needed to know.

Sihan'el didn't speak, merely shifted to almost launch himself onto Hela, pressing her back down on the bedroll, on top of the blankets, pulling her hands above her head even as he leaned over her, one leg pinning both of hers still. "So, you want strength, challenge? You might have bitten off too much, though this will show that, Hela." He shifted his grip to have both of her wrists in his hand, then braced himself and lowered his head to her mouth. There was no resistance, only eyes bright with eagerness, eagerness which he could smell permeating much more than her expression. The benefit, or detriment, of having holo'nil'talq was the sensitivity of the senses, and learning many things that were not the subject of conversations merely by paying attention to those senses.

Her mouth was clearly hungry for his, and she only tugged a bit at how her arms were for her own comfort, comfort he allowed her, for now. When he raised his head, he could see the same helplessness she had a tenday ago, but it was different now. In addition to the helplessness was a strong satisfaction. He wanted to test that, to see if it would be enough for his agreement.

"Yes," she hissed, even as she stretched under him, catlike. The feel of her body pressed up against him, even with their clothes between them, excited him.
"Vaeh'lesk'rediv." *Desire proven.* He couldn't help but grin at her awkward use of the Old Tongue.

He pulled his belt off with one hand, then wrapped it around her wrists, tightly enough to remind her that she had almost entirely asked for this. Then, pulling his hand back down to rest at her shoulder, he looked down at his lover and deliberately reached for the ties of her own belt, something that currently stood in the way of how he'd handle things. "Yes, in full view, should someone come looking. You want pride. You'll get that. But we'll see if this agreement can be reached. I intend to get that yes of yours much louder, a scream perhaps, before my agreement is given."

There wasn't fear in her eyes. Probably she knew that he wasn't going to harm her, only prove his power with her for now. As his fingers found skin along her belly, he could hear gasps. Well, if she enjoyed that, he could imagine having fun with those reactions for quite some time. With a bit of determination, he focused on what he intended. One way or another, his decision would be reached tonight. And it seemed that it might be a positive one.

Chapter 7

Ranor was quietly discussing news from home with Redel when the cries startled half of the camp. It wasn't yet nighttime, but Ranor was very aware of what those cries were. Even as his companion moved to reach for his sword, Ranor shook his head. "I know that voice, and I can tell you that she's not in pain. Rather, I imagine the opposite."

Redel blinked, then lowered his hand, "You're suggesting that she and Sihan'el are working out their issues? Perhaps a little startling, but probably for the best. I hope you're right on the nature of those sounds, though." As a second cry burst out, this one clearly in Trade, and a verbal affirmative to something, he shook his head and laughed, "I suspect you're right. She wouldn't use Trade in this camp without good reason."

Ranor chuckled, then nodded, "That's definitely Aunt Hela's voice. I've heard it long enough to know. As to what should be done about it? I'd say give them about a half-candlemark before we go to investigate, though I suspect that we might both want to do so, together. With those sounds, I'd think that they might need my services. And if that son of yours is at all intelligent, he'll be wanting some form of agreement first. If not, it should be suggested before dealing with the issue at hand."

"You're that skeptical about her motives? And you've known her far longer than I have. I wonder what your Goddess says about this, since it likely will reverse the order of the usual bonds."

Ranor grinned, "Jirel would probably merely be amused. There are many cases where the consummation preceded the binding, though rarely that close in time. Railah may be much more strict about things, but neither of the two is Railahn, so that doesn't matter. And it might simplify things a bit when we do bring this before her father and grandfather. I'm not going to be the one to do so, and I'm going to heavily hint to Rhiann that this should wait on the pair themselves rather than news brought ahead."

Redel seemed to agree, and that made things much easier. They waited, still exchanging news about what had been done in the interim until things had been quiet for quite a while. Then Ranor nodded in the direction he'd heard the screams from. "Let's take our time, as they may still be recovering, but I hope you can manage to not be too hard on them, Redel."

"It would be hard to be any gentler with the issue than I've been. I almost threw him at her when his mind started calling those constructs. I've worked with them both. I think that this might be the best solution, and if you consider where I have to stand on it, I'm giving them as much leeway as I possibly can."

They made their way amid the tents and outcroppings of this little canyon until they found the open ground where Sihan'el and Hela were. It looked like they probably could have given the pair more time and mayhap should have. Hela was still lying on the bedroll, on top, rather than within, though she was now properly clothed, except for the belt that Sihan'el was fastening. His own clothes were slightly less placed, mostly because his belt was tied rather tightly around her wrists. He looked up and seemed very wary. Hela looked like she wanted to give a tongue lashing to anyone who dared question how she ended up in this situation.

Redel looked over the situation, put his hands behind his back, just forward of the tip of SkySong, and shook his head with a faint smile. "I should hope that there was at least permission involved. If not, I am available for justice, though I'd suggest you both be careful what you ask of that."

Sihan'el reached up and tugged the belt free, then fastened it around his own waist, tucking up the loosened trousers that were under the edge of his tunic. Then he gave a good hard look at Hela before backing up. "I can't exactly answer that one, Hela."

Hela rubbed at her wrists, then narrowed her eyes at Redel, almost as if she expected him to be an enemy in this. "Except for the bond, he was given fairly wide permission. And considering what I'd asked from him recently, I'm not going to complain about that, either." Her voice sounded a little testy, as if challenging anyone to argue against her.

Ranor shifted his vision into determining health. Neither had any injuries outside of the stiffness those arms likely had. Indeed, they looked like whatever they'd been up to had dealt with most of the harmful stress they'd been carrying when he'd last seen them. "Well, it looks like the two of you might have come to some sort of agreement during that time. Are you ready to tell us what it is so that we can help you deal with it? I'd volunteered my services yesterday. That's still very much a possibility. So long as there's no ill will between the two of you any longer."

Sihan'el looked nervously at Hela, then nodded, trying to regain the power he had likely had only moments before they'd arrived. And Ranor was inclined to think that it was a lot of power. Hela respected power. It would make sense that anything that got her to that level of excitement, as understood by her cries, would take a great deal of strength and pride. There was also the fact that the words that Ranor could identify clearly from Hela's cries were affirmations of some sort. Then, somehow, from his nervousness, Sihan'el seemed to make a decision.

"Actually, we might be needing both of you, Father, Cousin. I think it best to have Father's help first before I make what could be a very major mistake."

Ranor laughed and glanced at Redel, "I suspected he was smart. This proves it."

Redel inclined his head, "So, the two of you have reached a decision to make this partnership last, beyond what we're doing now. That might be for the best, but I agree with Ranor. A formal agreement would be wise, especially as, though Hela was raised in the west where love matches occur frequently, she's never seemed inclined toward that, but rather to games of power. Making sure that whatever agreement you do come to is held is probably a good idea. And I expect that Hela might find it to her advantage to bind my son in the same way."

Sihan'el seemed taken aback by that, almost like he hadn't expected such a ready agreement. Ranor decided to help him out a bit. "So, Sihan'el, since you're the one who spoke up on this, what terms are you asking of my aunt? What is it you want her to agree to?"

The young man took a deep breath, then closed his eyes for a moment, a sign that he was thinking. "The first thing, and perhaps most important, was an offer she made before this got rather interesting." He coughed a moment. "She agreed to accept as her own any children of mine that show up, either my son Vashk if he still lives, or any other I don't know about, and there could be more. Beyond that, I want her bound to honor the bond, since it has been offered as bond of earth. She can't just decide that she's bored and go elsewhere. I have real reason to believe that's possible. Otherwise, I don't think there's anything I can demand from her."

Redel nodded, then glanced at Hela. "Are those terms agreeable to you, Cousin? And do you have any of your own? I suspect you do, but I'd suggest you think carefully before making requests that put this out of balance."

Hela seemed to have recovered more quickly, at least from the shock of finding her nephew and cousin walking up at such a time. "I see your point, Redel. One thing that should be agreed upon is that he also cannot just walk away when he's bored or gets an opportunity he sees is better. Beyond that, I would like his assistance with my work. He might not choose to serve the Serpent Lord, though that may come in time, but he should be willing to assist me as necessary."

Redel glanced back at Sihan'el, who merely nodded. Then the knight drew his soulsword in a swift motion, embedding the tip in the ground before him. "I think, since Hela is more familiar with this ritual than Sihan'el, she should make her promise first, to give him a better idea of what's going on. As a warning to you, Son, this type of promise cannot be broken without correction from the Goddess. So be very careful what you promise."

Ranor stepped back as Hela righted herself, then moved to kneel next to the blade, placing a hand upon it and speaking a very carefully worded version of the promise Sihan'el had asked for. It was complete, which was good. There wouldn't be any room for her to wiggle out of those sparse requirements. Then Sihan'el got up and repeated the situation, seeming a little nervous about the last part, that he would help Hela with her duties, but he didn't back out of any of it. There must have been a shock from the soulsword, because he was almost flinching as he pulled his hands away.

Ranor glanced around. "Well, we could try rounding up the rest of the family, but I think you two may be a little too exhausted from your activities to handle much searching. And this is best done now, I think. As a warning, however, I will not be bringing word of this to either Grandfather Maran or Grandfather Arandel. I'll be trying to explain to Rhiann why he shouldn't either. It should fall in your control, and honestly, neither one can do much of anything once the binding is done. It's legally binding, which limits what Grandfather Arandel can do, and Grandfather Maran would be more concerned about Hela's reputation being saved by the bond between you. If you're ready, I can perform it here and now. I don't need to ask for vows, since you've both given them in a very powerful way. I just need to perform the ritual, sealing the two of you together."

It didn't take long, especially as neither Hela nor Sihan'el was in much of any condition to argue. The seed energized and planted, and a nod of approval from Redel, and it was done. Perhaps in more definite ways than Redel had ever expected. The bit with the sword-oaths was well thought out, better than merely using him as a mediator. As they stood up, wiping fresh earth off of their clothes, Ranor nodded, "I'd suggest, Hela, that you remove this bedroll back to where the rest of the company are camping. I wouldn't want to suggest that either of you lack the comfort of each other's arms tonight, though I don't know if you'll have energy for more just yet."

Sihan'el seemed still rather abashed at how he'd been caught but didn't say anything at all. Hela was likely the far more vocal one. And so, Ranor decided he had to give his aunt a little advice, things that she might not understand yet. "Aunt, you might not know it, but it took a lot for our cousin to allow this to happen. He might be looking away right now, but that's because he just gifted you with something precious to him, and he's not sure that you'll take the care of it that he would like. If you're wise, you'll take the time now to go to him, acknowledge the gift he gave you, and reassure him that you mean his son no ill. It's hard for him to accept otherwise. And you are not like my son. You know that very well. Redel may not have had these children of his for very long, but there's little doubt that he loves them both and wants the best for them. He seems to have decided that you are the best chance Sihan'el has right now, but I think you should honor that with a show that you know what he just lost."

She stared at Ranor for just a moment, then decided that his advice was worth taking. As she moved over to Redel, inclining her head, Ranor could hear the soft words, "I will remember your aid, Father, and respect it. I have too much benefit from him to misuse him, no matter how callous you think I am."

Redel tilted his head, then reached out to pull Hela into perhaps the first hug she'd ever had from him. Ranor could hear whispers but didn't want to listen too closely. It was enough. There might be a mess at home because of this, but it would be solved. And perhaps solve other problems as well.

Chapter 8

Vishti could see how uncomfortable Kialor was at dinner. He'd come to her and praised what he saw of her fighting skills in practice, but seemed like he wanted to talk about something. And yet, nothing seemed to make the words come. His attention was focused on her, not her sister, but it still gave Vishti a great deal of worry. What could have come over Kialor, who had promised that he'd stay at her side, that he could not articulate what was on his mind? It made her nervous, wondering if something was being done again without her being informed.

After dinner, Kialor made it a point to take her to their place in the camp, even going so far as to hold her hand through the journey. If he was disturbed by the sounds of Hela's cries that went on, he didn't mention it. In fact, he seemed to be entirely ignoring anything to do with her brother and his aunt and had been for days. She wondered if that, too, was a part of it.

He gestured to the bedrolls but did not open them, instead making a wry smile. "Vishti, I think we need to talk, and it's not going to be easy on me, though not for the reasons that are likely popping into your mind. It has to do with my own honesty and things that were explained to me today that I have been very resistant to. If you'll sit, I'll try to make the words come, but they are very difficult for me, and I hope you'll be able to understand why."

That was cause enough for alarm. He wanted a serious discussion and indicated that things about his honesty were hard for him. His words made it sound like he might be breaking a promise, though he had tried to assure her that whatever he was doing, it was not for the reasons she was thinking of. She had a hard time sitting down, especially letting him talk. The fear of abandonment was very strong, and she wanted nothing more than to curl up and hide right now. But she needed him too much to argue. Not yet.

"What is it, Kialor? What has it been that's been worrying you all evening? I knew that there was something wrong, but you have not spoken of it at all."

He settled in across from her, placing one hand on her knee. "Vishti, this is nothing ill against you. In fact, quite the opposite. I want you to take a moment, try to remove those fears that I can see in your expression, in that gaze that won't meet mine. I'm not abandoning you, and I know that's your first fear. There's no way around the fact that you fear it, especially with other things going on. As my father said, you're afraid of losing everything, me, your brother, possibly your father. You feel that there's nothing left for you to hold onto, and it makes it difficult for you to share us, all of us, with those who need us. I can understand that, and even more what my father suggested. He knows more than any of us what happens when a woman has those fears and jealousy. And you can't deny that you're jealous of Sai'velk. You don't have to be, but you are, and I will accept that."

Those words made a difference. His first thought was to reassure her that he was not leaving her and acknowledge that he understood her fears, possibly better than she did. He'd mentioned the fact that she felt disconnected from her brother and that she might want more from her father too. She hadn't considered the latter, but there was a desire, when she looked for it, to be special to her father, someone he cared about. She wanted her relationship with him to mirror what she'd lost with her mother when the Sisters had taken her away. There was still a part of her, tiny at the moment, that wanted to have her mother back, though she wasn't sure if she wanted to listen to it.

"What is it that you wish to speak of if you are not wishing to hurt me, Kialor?"

"Vishti, I never want to hurt you. That's something that I'm not sure you understand yet. I want you whole, strong, and I asked for advice today because I realized I need to know how to help you get to that point. The problem for me, though, is that I'm less certain of what my father sees in me, perhaps what others see in me, than they are. I would like what they're suggesting to be true, but I don't know yet, and I'm not sure how to find out the truth. I don't like Father's idea of repeating something until it becomes true, but it might be the only way to get me past that hurdle. So, against my own better judgment, I'll try here. Because it's something you need to hear."

He clasped his hand over hers, then reached out with the other hand and cupped her chin. "I think I've discovered the beginnings of what I'd wanted before we married, Vishti. I wanted, when I married, for it to be for love. I wanted to feel that my partner was the most important part of my life and that I would do anything for them. In a way, that's already happened. I've found that I push myself harder to make sure you get through things. I constantly worry over your happiness and your strength. I want to be that strength, even if I don't feel adequate for the task. If that's what love is, perhaps that's indeed what I'm feeling. I can't be certain. Father thinks it's true. I think your father believes it is true too. I'm beginning to think that he wouldn't have allowed this to happen, our marriage, if he didn't think that I loved you on some level. It just might not be a level that I can see in myself yet."

Vishti couldn't help but look up at him in startlement. There was a tone of utter vulnerability in his voice, like he was opening himself up, ready to be harmed if she took offense. She only vaguely understood his concept of love and realized that, especially with how awkwardly he approached it, maybe he himself didn't understand it. But he, who prided himself on being very honest, was offering her something that she knew he considered extremely important. He was trying to offer her the deepest emotion he could imagine, and much of that was so that she could heal.

"Kialor," she breathed, "I do not understand the importance of this love, not the way you think on it, yet I am unsure of how to deal with what you say. It is beyond my knowledge, and I only know that you are trying to offer me something again."

He smiled wryly, tilting his head to look at her more carefully. "Vishti, I told you many times that I consider you very beautiful, in some ways moreso than your sister, because I can see what you've lived through, what you've overcome, and that strength that you have inside is one of the most beautiful things in life. I know that I've been reluctant at times to give you the touch you crave, partly because I have a hard time not thinking that such touch will harm you and remind you of the darkness you've passed through. I want to know that what I'm doing is something you enjoy, though you've never had a complaint about that touch. I do desire you, can't help but do so, but I am more concerned about how you feel about it, what it brings up in your mind. I only want joy in your spirit, never sorrow or fear. I just don't know how to make that come true."

Vishti could feel almost like something was swelling to burst within her. He was so honest, so intent, and his words told her that he wanted nothing but good for her. That he held himself back because of his fears, fears that his actions might bring her back to the darkness that she had escaped. She could feel trickles of dampness in the corners of her eyes and shook unexplainably. She didn't understand what she was feeling. It didn't have a name that she could think of. Or perhaps it did, and she just had never experienced it to know how to define it. Whatever, she knew that she was overwhelmed at the moment.

Somehow, he understood. He moved to his knees, put his hands behind her back, and gently laid her down on the bedroll. Then he bent over her, lowering his face to hers, not with strong passion, but something softer, deeper. It was a kiss that made her alternate between shrinking within and being too full of whatever feeling she had to control herself. Her hands moved to his sides, trying desperately to communicate what was in her head and heart.

Kialor pulled himself up and smiled down at her. "Vishti, dear Vishti, we'll figure this out. You don't have to fear me leaving you. I won't do that, and not just because I gave you my word, but because you are that important to me. I enjoy seeing your smile in the mornings and feeling your hands reaching out to me at random times, just for the comfort of my presence. I know that this is rather overwhelming for you. It is for me too. But, just maybe, it's what we both need, to acknowledge to each other that there is something here beyond promises, beyond the danger that we're facing together. We need to know that we feel strongly about each other. I think that's true from you and has been for a while. I just needed to come to a point where I could admit it of myself. And that wasn't easy."

He gestured to one side of the bedroll, "Should I help you roll into this? I doubt I'm half as good at making a woman squeal with enjoyment as your brother seems to have proven himself today, but I think we both need comfort. It should start out merely holding each other, and let's see what our hearts want. I think perhaps that's a good first step."

Vishti glanced at him and realized something in amusement. "You have desire too."

"I do, a lot, but I've been afraid that, without proper feeling, I was doing you wrong, Vishti. Tonight, though, seeing you like this, I think that feeling is beginning to come out of hiding. But I'm not going to rush either the desire or the emotion; just try to take you as I find you and hopefully find myself in the process."

She couldn't disagree with that and moved to invest herself in the bedrolls. Perhaps things weren't nearly as bad as they had seemed. Even remembering Sai'velk's presence didn't bring up feelings of bitterness and anger. All it required had been his honest feelings, and she was certain she'd seen that already.

Chapter 9

Sihan'el was surprised to find the peaceful priest Rhiann suggesting that they ride together for this part of the journey. Ostensibly, it was to give the horses more of a chance to rest on the path. They still only had eight beasts, one of which did not have a proper saddle, only a pack saddle, and she carried supplies for a day or so. Switching which horses carried double, and frequent rests, made a lot of sense, considering that their party had increased by half-again. But Rhiann was almost always allowed to ride. His movements were hindered far greater than anyone else's, and their speed was significantly slowed when he did walk, for that false foot of his was not good for walking quickly.

Rhiann was the expert here, and though he still needed help to mount, he was the one controlling the stallion that was Sihan'el's usual mount. His horsemanship was quite good, even if the weight of both of them on the horse might mean a rest far sooner than there would otherwise be. But it seemed that the Ollahmic priest had reason to arrange this. For no sooner than they'd gotten started than Rhiann's voice came back to him, soft, but controlled, the voice of a Singer.

"I don't think Uncle Maran ever thought to live to see the day that Hela would choose to settle down, though I'm not sure that's actually her intent, or yours. But it will both comfort him and give him reason to worry for quite some time, once he knows. I do agree with Ranor, however, that this news should best come from the two of you, not Ranor and myself when we return. I'm just hoping that what you're doing is for the best. Your father seems to think so, and Ranor agrees, apparently, but neither of them really know you well. And your father's interactions with Hela were extremely limited. Which means that perhaps I should help lay down some groundwork to make sure that what you did does not become a mistake."

"So now I get another elder Calasti judging me?" Sihan'el couldn't help the annoyance in his tone, though he almost immediately regretted it, not because Rhiann was a threat, but because of how the Singer handled himself.

"Still just as sharp as when Nefta brought you and Maskar back, almost coming to blows even while Evanira lay weak and recovering from what had been done to her? I may not know you, but I did raise two sons of my own, and can be proud enough of them. I also helped Maskar through his hardest times, times when he had to admit to weaknesses every bit as big as the ones I imagine you have. You seem to, at least a little, pity your sister Vishti. What he'd been through was every bit as bad. The marks aren't on his face, but clear in a brand on the inside of his ankle. I think, though your sister might not believe it, that you have internal scars, if not external. And in that, maybe you just need a good listener, someone who won't judge you, won't think you any less because of where you've been. I think you'll heal better if you get a chance to unleash all of that bitterness you have within you. And I think that it might make the situation you got yourself into day before yesterday a little less likely to bite you unexpectedly."

Rhiann's voice was completely calm, soft and gentle, and Sihan'el realized that it was all too easy to misjudge this priest. Where Hela was prickly all over and full of pride, and Kialor tended more toward introspection, there was something much more nurturing in Rhiann. The priest didn't look back, and seemed to have only volunteered a non-judgmental ear for now. Whether that might haunt him later, Sihan'el didn't know, but suspected it probably wouldn't. At least as long as no one else was listening in.

"What can I tell you, Cousin, that you don't already know? I'm sure my father gave you enough background on what it's like to be raised among the Sisterhood. It was different for me than my sisters, doubtless. They were women, and thus recognized as superior. I hadn't reached what I gather is age of adulthood in the west when I was first called to serve. While you'd expect someone raised among assassins to be called to kill, that was not my purpose, and that was made readily clear. I was lucky, perhaps. I know that Vedask's situation was different. He was let to mature a bit more, and then ended up being passed among some of the less than pleasant Sisters, a toy for their pride. Me, well, Vishti's mother thought that I might be able to serve the resistance. She decided that the best way to gauge my subtlety and loyalty required me being exposed a little early to certain things. It was pleasant. I won't deny that, but I knew that I was controlled. And, at that time, I didn't see any likelihood of that ever changing."

"After you'd been recruited, I imagine a few things changed, didn't they?" Rhiann said nothing about the pain, especially the mention to Sihan'el's dead brother. He merely seemed to approach this as if it were normal dinner conversation. That made it easier, somehow.

"They did. It began a bit of a tug between the two groups. I was actually used to try to get information quickly, ply it out of certain of the more loyal Sisters with service and pleasure. A lot of that was less than pleasant, but I was considered very good at what I was doing. Sah'lev'da'kril made sure that there were enough signs of appreciation for my work that I didn't question it much. I learned a lot, studied what I could in the meantime, and managed to even get myself assigned to help ferry messages between the fortress and certain outlying places. Never too far. Perhaps the Mayisna was yet uncertain of how loyal Father was. Or she could possibly have suspected me. I don't know. But I was luckily away from the Fortress when the Mayisna saw what Father did to one of the Elder Sisters. And, from what I gather, she did see, from that Sister's eyes, through the tah'nel. I was told that it was enough of a shock to the Great Mother's mind that she was delirious for a time. When she recovered, her anger knew no bounds."

Rhiann nodded, "I might know a little better than you would what caused that shock. Your father told me the story while he was still getting used to his soulsword. He said that the Sister in question had used a very damaging magic, one that would have made his own weapons useless. When his sister's familiar creature brought the unpaired soulsword to him, in the middle of the fight, he took the chance, thinking only to use something that could not be damaged. That's when the change happened, and that's when Sacred Sword Zedaia's powers became helpful. She'd managed to let Grandfather Tainen appear visibly, and he told your father that he could absorb magic with the blade. The rest, well, your father learned that quite on accident. Having absorbed the spells that the Sister had placed, he moved to kill her, and ended up discharging that magic unexpectedly. It was a surprise to him, as she exploded into a shower of residue that coated a large area. There was nothing left of her afterward. To be connected with someone mentally as they die like that, yes, that would send almost anyone into severe shock."

Sihan'el took a moment to absorb that. Father's betrayal of the Mayisna had come so suddenly, and had been such a personal strike, since the Great Mother had been watching through the Sister's eyes, that that alone could explain the period of madness. Considering that she'd been insane before, it merely pushed her that much further along the path to bringing destruction to her own people.

Sihan'el spoke softly, once he'd thought it through. "I don't know what to make of Father, honestly. I'd been told he was a fool, long ago. Now that I've met him, he doesn't seem to make sense. He stands for law and justice, specifically the laws of his adopted home, and yet he's actually encouraged what lies between Hela and myself. I know that if I do break one of those laws, the punishment is likely to be swift, no matter who I am, and yet, well, he seems to be pushing me toward a situation which is very unlike what he stands for. He said that Railah would not be a good choice for me to serve, if I serve anyone. He doesn't chastise me, or do anything I'd expect. And that leaves me largely confused."

Rhiann seemed to have an answer for that too. "When your father was finally uncovered, after a great deal of fear and anger within the town over the seemingly unfindable assassin who we knew was there, well, he expected death. He was prepared at least to be imprisoned. What happened was very different. His father, Uncle Jalak, walked into the place where he held Maskar and Evanira, alone, and stated that all he wanted to do was talk. Your father had already come to heavily respect my Uncle Jalak, even if he hadn't identified himself yet as Jalak's son. It was a meeting that would change Redel forever, I think, because he found out that love overcomes almost everything. When he came before Grandfather Arandel in judgment, he expected that Grandfather would not be allowed mercy. He found out that it is quite the opposite. Your father took that to the extreme. He willingly admits his failures, his errors in judgment, and the crimes that Railah absolved him of. And, in doing so, he offers an opportunity to bring others to work with him. He is more of a peacemaker than Grandfather can claim, honestly, and it's made him very good in handling the job he was given. His first effort is always to find out what would most help the people he's working with. If there's a way to make that work, he'll do that. That's what he's doing with you. He's looking not for his own benefit, but yours. And, it seems, your wife's."

Sihan'el wasn't sure what to make of that revelation. It answered a great many things, things that hadn't made any sense before. And it gave him a new perspective of just what kind of man his father was. "He never said any of that to me. Maybe I would have listened more if he had. I've found that I do want to work with him. He's offered me chances I know I wouldn't get elsewhere. I just don't know how to do that best."

"Perhaps, at some point, you should sit down and talk with him, share your stories together. You have more in common than you think, and I suspect you'll find him a staunch ally if you handle it right. He almost had to kill both Ma'enda and La'halsi. La'halsi was drugged by something that was killing her, and through a linked tah'nel, Ma'enda, very painfully. If Maskar's idea of how to heal them both hadn't worked, it would have been a race between your father and my nephew to see who could offer them that final mercy. He probably hurts very deeply inside to know that there was a child he will never meet, one who died out here in the battle against the Great Mother. It makes him want even more to do what's right for the children he does have. If you have any doubts about what's similar between the two of you, consider that he does know, very well, what you're going through about your own son. If you need comfort from that, he'd give it, willingly. Just remember, you aren't alone. It's not even you and Hela against the world. It only requires remembering that you have things in common with others to find you allies. Even in the most unexpected places."

Sihan'el listened to that, and realized that it was true. He hadn't expected anything like this from Ollahm's priest, but the advice came naturally. He decided to accept it. "I will try to talk to Father. I think I understand him enough now not to feel threatened by him."

"That's what I want to hear, Cousin. It means that my time was not wasted. Though it rarely is when someone's hurting like you are." The tone was so comfortable, reassuring, that Sihan'el decided that he liked Rhiann, possibly quite a bit.

Chapter 10

Maskar and Dastyl stood in the middle of a chamber clearly intended for complex castings, perhaps one of the oldest such places, beyond the two Earth-bowels that Maskar was aware of. Kialor had discussed enough of the background for what they were doing with Maskar that he was aware at least a little about the nature of how such powerful Musics were once done. It still sounded very iffy to him, and yet, he was going to need to be a central part of this, if for no other reason than because he was able to link into the web that the divine council needed to somehow connect with.

"I'm going to make sure that all questions are answered, at least as fully as we can manage, before we get into the working. I've talked to each of you privately, tried to make sure that everyone knows what their part in this would be, but it's now time to share insights among the whole group. We really only have one chance at this, because if we don't do it right, well, saying that bad things will happen is perhaps a gross understatement. Yes, this is going to be extremely difficult, as among us, we have a total of four fully trained Singers, and six whose experience with this is extremely limited. Well, limited in Singing altogether. Aside from myself and Redel, none of the rest of you have even touched the world's harmonies before."

Kialor couldn't help but be amused at how Maskar was handling things. Doubtless the reason Dastyl was standing with him had mostly to do with the fact that the Scholar had more information on ancient resonant practices than even the other Singers beyond Maskar, and because this was indeed his place, a location that he and his people had kept, even with all of the dangers that this world had in it. Yet, for reasons of his experience with Great Musics, Maskar was the one who had to lead the discussion. He also knew far better than anyone else how to communicate these concepts in terms that would make them possible to comprehend for the non-Singers.

Vishti moved forward, hesitantly, as if she were far weaker than she would need to be to pull this off. "You still say that I must power this Music. That it is because of my connection with the world that I am both protected and necessary. Why did the messenger who brought the others not bring one who knows how to do this? Surely she would be better than I would in such a position."

Kialor moved up behind her, making sure to give her the physical touch she needed to keep strong. Her question was a valid one, and theoretically could make this have a little greater chance of success than it did with her at the central position. But he only knew that the gods had brought two people to this place alone, Rhiann and Father. Doubtless, if the gods had thought that Virea was better, they would have brought her, and possibly Leltorin, if only so that the Music had what it needed to work properly.

Maskar inclined his head. "We left Sharlan knowing that this sort of thing was possible, Vishti. We knew that there might need to be something very powerful. It's why I came. But right now, I suspect that there are very good reasons for why you must be the one to handle this task. I don't know what all of them are, though I would hazard a guess that part of it is that the Risen One needs Leltorin to stay on that side of the mountains. Possibly because of what he carries. If something should go wrong, and it could, there might be no way to get that token back where it belongs. And he can't leave it behind. Just as it is not safe for Virea to spend much time apart from him. It's a balancing act with the two of them, and I know some of the potential consequences. And, aside from Virea, the only other person beyond yourself who can manage this working would be our enemy, and you know full well that she wouldn't even consider it. So, it must fall to you. I know it's hard, but it's something we have to do. If I had another answer, I'd use it. But I haven't been able to come up with one, and this offers us a chance. If we can all work together long enough to handle it."

Sihan'el moved up on Vishti's other side, taking her hand and squeezing it. "I won't be far away, Vishti. Just as Kialor won't be. And, what's more, I can contact you, in some way, if things go wrong. That's something that I don't think his sister has. I won't be involved in anything but focusing on you, feeding you what I can of my own strength to power it. Hela understands, agrees even. She's known for a while that, while she may now be my wife, you've had a claim much longer."

Dastyl nodded, speaking in a low voice. "Having a connection like that increases our likelihood of success. Even as the dah'ral and I must contain the force, stabilize it, it makes sense that the one who must power it has other succor. Especially if he does not need to touch her to grant that succor. I believe it was indicated that that might be the case? Touching her during this would be fraught with danger."

Hela spoke up, looking at the other god-touched in the room. "So, what we're supposed to do is somehow merge our patrons' energy with this net that Kialor will be handling? I don't really understand much more than that, though you say that it will almost be instinctive when we're doing it."

Kialor cleared his throat. "More precisely, Aunt, you'll be focusing that energy into a link that I can grasp with my gifts and Song. I will be connecting those to the web, though, as you said, it's more theory now than actual Song as such. We'll be working in something completely unknown to all of us, even Maskar, though he's done things of this level before. I really wish I weren't the one to do this, but, honestly, I don't think that either Aunt Selah or Uncle Telin could manage this, even if they can now touch this web. It has to do with how we're focused, really. There are things they'll always be better at than I am, gifts I will never attain, even. On the reverse, I think I have a vague idea now, at least, of what my Lady asks of her priests. I can't really explain it, but this does fit among those duties."

Suddenly Sai'velk spoke up, a tremor in her voice, "You seem quite content with the dangers in this, but what will happen to the world if we fail?"

Maskar shrugged, shook his head. "I can't say. I'd like to say that the divine council will find some way to change things to allow the world to survive. You could ask your god, or ask any of the others here to ask theirs, to see what might have been put in place should we fail. They're likely not investing all of their energy into you for this. I can't imagine anyone being able to hold that much power, and the gods aren't stupid. They doubtless know the risks, and have been planning this almost since the time I came up with the idea. But, for myself, I don't know what might happen. I just know, without an attempt, we're probably dooming the world. What Mi'la has done to those constructs has made them very dangerous. That danger may not be immediate, but the longer we wait, the less likely we'll have a chance to pick up the pieces and try something else if this fails. So, we act now, while we have everyone together. And while I have the courage to face what I know will be the result of this. It's not a pretty picture for me, probably not for Aunt Denora either. Part of me doesn't want this to work, but I'm going to try nonetheless."

Kialor winced at the still very clear venom that Maskar held for anything from the Heavens. It not only meant that Maskar wasn't going to play nice to the gods once this was finished. It could very well spell doom to the working itself, if only because doubts would almost certainly become magnified in the process. The fact that he was torn two directions would mean that his focus would not be wholly upon the success. Introducing a will toward failure was not a good thing, at least not from what he understood of such magics.

Rhiann spoke up, his voice carrying even though he did not seem to raise it. "Maskar, in this, you and the Scholar must set aside your hatreds for a day. You can do so, though it is unpleasant for you. You worked with my daughter when you needed to, to protect Evanira. You can do it again, because she, like the rest of the world, depends on your focus. So do Brehl and Yossa. Do not go into this with anger, with the memory of what you believe was betrayal, in your heart. A great part of what we need is a focus on life, on our connection with the world. Though you choose no faith, you are very much a part of that world, and can represent it as a mortal, even as Scholar Dastyl can. If you want a place for those who are not god-touched in this world, it is up to you to make that place. Come to the council with a willingness to bargain, not to merely stalk off in hate. The success or failure might depend on your own willingness to compromise."

It wasn't a trick of the lighting. Maskar did turn even paler, though Kialor hadn't thought that possible. There was a sound that gave the young priest a guess as to what Maskar was thinking. Then there was a nod, quietly. "You knew that you're the only one I'd let say those things to me, didn't you, Uncle?"

"I knew that you have wisdom, when you need it, Maskar. Sometimes it just takes the right nudge. If my words are that nudge, then I consider them well spent. I know your pain. I know how much this is costing you. But it is worth it. Or it will be worth it if you spend yourself in it the way I know you can. Will you let down that pride, even for the duration of this Music? Acknowledge that perhaps there were reasons that you don't know for what happened. Perhaps, when this is done, you can find out those reasons, if you are willing to speak with the one person who can answer you fully. You haven't been, through all these years. He waits. I'm certain of that."

It was as if there was a battle going on, though no voices were raised, and no threats made. It was a battle that existed within Maskar, and the tension was palpable. Finally, inclining his head, Maskar admitted defeat, not by his Uncle, but by his greater self. "If we succeed, then I'll consider it. If I don't, well, you won't demand anything, but I know how disappointed you'll be."

"You should be more concerned with disappointing yourself, Nephew. But I will be content with any progress you make here." It was gentle, almost like a salve being put on a wound. That was ever Rhiann's way. And it was a way that seemed to always get results.

Chapter 11

Vishti took her place in the center of the room, her hands on a crystal that Maskar had taken several candlemarks to attune. It seemed to throb, not only in her hands, but somewhere within herself, too. This was something she was afraid of, terrified of, in many ways. She had been told, during the greatest part of her life, that to open herself up to a crystal was highly dangerous, not only to herself, but to others. She could do so much, but so much of it was uncontrolled. She knew the basis of what she was doing, taking up a sense of the earth itself, and holding it in a state where Kialor could connect the strength of each of the six deities. It had been decided that he would link Lady Night in last, because that would be completely his, and it would be dangerous for him to be channeling her energy throughout the ritual. He'd said that he'd take it at the end, just long enough to link it into what needed to be done. He seemed to have courage, where she did not.

But maybe that was one of the few illusions he allowed himself. He would do what he needed to, regardless of his fear. In a way, no matter how scared he was, there were things more important to him than his own safety, even his own sanity. She knew he'd been trying to say that she was one of those things, and, for now, she was willing to try to believe it. She just didn't know how that would work when the force of life itself was channeled through her, in her body and mind and soul, all at once. Maskar had warned her that it would be difficult, that, when working much the same way, Virea had almost been overcome by the thought of giving up that power. He said he thought that it might be different with Vishti, because she had never been allowed to hold power over much of anything, and, because of that, might not understand its allure at this point.

She looked around at the members she could see, four out of the six in the first ring around her, one of the three in the outer ring. But that one also made a difference to her. It was her brother, and he'd said that his job in this was merely to be here for her. He would be focusing his nature to strengthen hers. Perhaps, in that, he could do more than anyone else. If he could keep her sane, provide her with an anchor to the world she knew, maybe she'd survive this. But it seemed like there was little choice now in what she must do.

Closing her eyes, trying to focus, she started the first layer of harmonics. In a way, Maskar was right. In addition to the basis for the tune that was provided in this crystal, her own instincts would guide her. Indeed, Maskar wasn't sure that his guidance was the best. It was merely there to help her get started, since she'd never done any real resonant magic herself before. He was certain she could do it, and, only after she'd gotten the first few notes out, did she understand why. As her mind slipped into the awareness of the Song, she realized that her linking was natural, something very much a part of her. She didn't understand how that could be, but had to trust that she would continue to know, in the same way she had to trust that the others would feel their places the same way. It was different from what most Singers did. It was deeper, more creative. But it also made her more vulnerable.

Almost as soon as she'd started her song, she could hear two male voices ring out, full and rich, carrying the first of the wards that would protect the participants. That was Maskar's job, and Dastyl's. It was only after that music had stabilized that the others began singing. First came Ranor, representing Jirel. She was said to be the oldest, one who had been immortal even before she became a god. Then Hela's voice started singing, representing Vythen, who was the first to understand what needed to be done. She lost track as voice after voice wove itself into the reality that she was holding. Soon she was aware of nothing more than the realities of the earth that she had submerged herself in. It was a place of light and beauty, but also of darkness and fear. There was pain and pleasure, life and death. It surrounded her, filled her, made her something else for a time.

Memories crept into the song, memories of what she'd been, who she'd been. She remembered her betrayal, and also the loving gentleness of when Kialor first kissed her, to give her the languages she needed. She realized that this wasn't what she thought she'd be doing, what she thought she'd be feeling. She couldn't separate her own realities from what was being woven into the world. She couldn't make it just the world. For, now, in a real way, the world was her.

Almost like a lapping of a river came another voice, one long familiar. It was gentle, like the caresses she'd gotten from Kialor the night he told her that he thought perhaps he loved her. It soothed her, made her focus on the memories of pleasure, of hope. It took her a long moment to realize that that was Sihan'el, trying to help her regain her focus. Somehow, in the midst of the almost chaos of voices and power, he had known what she was doing, what she was feeling. He merely placed himself, mentally, where she knew that she would have succor.

It was very strange, holding onto his image in her mind, when so much was going on around her. She didn't even realize that she was still singing, only took the time to appreciate what he'd done for her, how much he'd given to protect her. She realized that a part of that was how he'd felt about her mother, someone who Vishti still hadn't made up her mind how she wanted to feel about. She knew, objectively, that it was her mother who'd initiated him into certain activities, certain pleasures. That did not bother her, not really, for Sah'lev'da'kril was not his mother, and the ways of the kril'dga were much different from how people thought in the west. But it brought sadness, to realize that she might have given up her last chance to find peace with someone she had once loved.

It was almost as if Sihan'el were kissing her cheek, drying her tears. Almost like they were physically close, even though there was a distance between them. He encouraged her with his Song, with his connection through her tah'nel. He tried to show that, no matter what happened, he had always loved her, wanted her to be happy. Even if her mother had encouraged it, Sihan'el had not needed that encouragement to be at her side, to help her heal from what had been done to her. He felt he'd owed that to her, even though their mothers were different, and, at that time, they did not know their father, did not even have his name. Or at least she had not. He might have, but he didn't speak of it. He only acknowledged that bond between them, made it real where it might otherwise have not been so.

Vishti opened her eyes for only a moment, seeing flashes as things were being done in the magical mindscape she'd created. But she realized that she could barely feel any of it. Nothing seemed to touch her herself save Sihan'el's song, his love. It was probably very different from what the other Singer, Virea, had felt when she'd done a Great Music. It was more open, less intrusive. While Vishti was aware that, in a real way, she was the earth itself during this, it did not diminish her at all to have someone else control her, it. She only knew that she had to hold it a little longer.

There was a message to Sihan'el's song, beyond strengthening her, taking away the pain that had troubled her for so long. It was a message that coaxed her out of her reverie in a subtle way. *We must put a part of ourselves into this, make ourselves a part of the world around us. That's what Maskar told us, and Singer Rhiann. We are as much a part of the web we're weaving as the gods we're linking into the world. We are the ones who will manifest this, and, because of that, we must place a part of our nature into the working.*

Vishti had to make a choice. She knew that instinctively, even as the connections were nearing their end. What was it that she would give to the world, what part of her nature was she going to plant into reality, nurture and make grow? She hadn't really thought of it before, not seriously. She'd known that she needed to give something, but she couldn't decide, could barely bare to think about what they would be doing. And yet, the Music would not complete without these personal gifts, these flashes of insight that would rework much of reality into hopefully a better place.

She realized that she didn't know what Sihan'el could give, besides the pain and hate he'd learned from always being a servant. Maskar, too, held old wounds, things that he couldn't let go of. Hela seemed to have little that was nurturing in her. Thus, Vishti's gift must be one of life, of healing. She tried to focus on that, to strengthen the tie she had to what had been done.

She remembered the priest, Leltorin, and how he gently tipped that cup to her lips, bringing her soothing relief from all that she'd been through, if only for a few moments. It healed the wounds, removed most of the scars, but it could not touch her soul. She remembered Kialor, gently tending her injuries, before that, making sure that they had not torn, even carrying her from the stables to the temple, because he was certain that she could not handle the walk. Those were her memories of healing, of salvation, in a way. And they gave her a seed that she would plant in this music, something that would perhaps make the pain go away in time. She focused on the biggest thing that Kialor had wished from her. She focused on the forgiveness, the acceptance that life wasn't always what we wanted, but always what we needed. She focused on the words of Maskar, that even our pains teach us things that we can use to aid others. Wrapping this seed in her song, she let loose the full power of the Music, opening her eyes to glance at Kialor opposite her, though in the first ring surrounding her. He nodded, seeming weary. She let loose the music, let it fall from their voices. It was done.

Chapter 12

Hela wasn't sure what it was that Kialor was doing, only knew that it was a part of what she needed to connect to. She could hear Vishti's voice, and Maskar's, but almost everything else was too chaotic to understand. She concentrated, when the time came for her to join into the Music, and tried to open herself as a channel for the Dread Lord's power. And, almost as quickly, she regretted it.

Perhaps it was merely Vythen's nature, the focus of his power, but it lanced through her painfully, seeming to burn her from the inside out. Like her acid had burned more than one man who'd dared too much, including the man who was now her husband. The pain had layers to it, as she tried to sort through the waves of agony to keep herself Singing. Her job would be the second done, and she hadn't imagined that Ranor might have gone through the same thing. It didn't make sense, not to her mind, only seemed to etch that agony through her, leaving her wondering if the Music would leave physical affects. Even as her ras'lah'tan would normally heal her, she realized that this might do more than she'd have any chance to overcome. She was strong, amazingly healthy, but it wasn't enough. Not nearly enough to overcome the torture of the connection.

~Child, there is a good reason that thou must be the one who bears my gift now,~ the god's words came to her despite the agony that she was feeling. ~Thou, more than any here beyond Maskar, can bear what must be done. I did not foresee it when I called thee to me, but this seems to be a great purpose for thee. Thou must endure, focusing the power of destruction, of death and pain, into the network. Both exist within thy people, but thou will connect what they bear with what I understand, that I may direct it more carefully. It is better the focused pain, the torment that thou endure, than the constant pointless harm that the enemy unleashes, even unto her own.~

So, it was the nature of his power, specifically, that was doing this to her. She was both relieved and annoyed. She had served him faithfully for more than a century, and yet, in this, he expected her to endure more than what he sent as his wrath against one who angered him. She had even managed to get Sihan'el's agreement to help her, when Lord Vythen demanded something that was beyond her. And it was quite likely that that would happen, should she live to survive this Music.

But then, she remembered one other Singer, the next to the last among the ones who would channel this divine power. He had endured much, and, according to Aunt Talina, even when his foot was being cut from him, he did not cry out. He'd forced himself to stand while enduring pain that would have caused a lesser man to faint, and had even managed a powerful music, not once, but twice. He had stayed on his feet longer than was healthy, and yet had only once since that point seemed even distressed by the liability of his false foot. If he could do this, she could. She could force her way through, because, no matter how much it hurt, she knew that she had to be at least as strong as Rhiann. Her cousin wasn't a fighter by nature, wasn't inured to suffering. She had to be able to do this, if only to prove that she was not his lesser.

Almost as she focused her will to keep channeling this power, she felt the pain lifted from her, taken from her grasp, and she realized that it had been woven into this web that Kialor was handling. She could see, now, what he'd been meaning, something about how the nature of the world was woven on a much finer level than she'd ever expected. She could see everyone, even with her eyes closed. She could see the way that the power changed, shifted, became something new. She had gotten past the worst of it.

Even as she became cognizant of these things, she could feel a light building opposite her, a golden-red light that filled and suffused her. It brought relief from the sense of burning that lay within her. It brought succor from the helplessness that had almost caused her to fail the ritual. Of course, that had to be Sai'velk. She served The Risen One, served the Phoenix, as she preferred to call the other brother god. She would be emitting renewal, almost bursting from within with the fires of purity. That purity was false in some ways. While Vythen would not claim any level of purity himself, Hela knew that the god of renewal had been just as responsible for the Godswar, perhaps even more, in some ways, because he had not had the compassion to try to imagine his brother as anything other than the cause of Lilal's suffering. He had only gained that compassion later, when he'd been able to see what his vendetta against Vythen had caused. And yet, for millennia, he had still considered only Vythen's part in the fight, not his own.

The light did not fade as Sai'velk relinquished the power into the web, a web that was growing brighter every moment. It would soon be Redel's turn, feeding the strength of Railah, the courage and determination, and judgment that were hers. It was only a moment of wondering to Hela as to how Railah's gift would manifest itself here before she could see it, again without opening her eyes to expose herself to the chaos of this magic. In some ways, it was like being buried alive. The influence of pure structure, pure law, felt almost like she'd been chained, locked away without any hope of freedom. A part of her fought this part of the music, tore at it in a way to preserve her autonomy.

Then, somewhere deep inside, she remembered how good it had felt to let Sihan'el bind her, to let him command, and to let him take what he would. She didn't understand that, but immersed herself in that feeling, the freedom that comes from relinquishing power. It had been an eye-opening experience the first time he'd had control, not the way he'd taken it with his belt around her wrists. She could understand, if only for a moment, why her mother, and her older sister, had both chosen submission, rather than power of their own. She could remember the pleasure of letting go, of not having to control everything. That knowledge and memory allowed her to move past Redel's gift to this web. It allowed her to breathe again, only to find that she hadn't stopped singing.

Rhiann's song was almost the opposite. Where Railah chained, Rhiann freed. Where she took command, he asked for suggestions. It was apparent in the music, even if there were no words that could be understood of it. He stood for Ollahm, the Lord of Bards, master of arts and crafts. While Ollahm and Railah were opposite in many ways, they still worked together, and it made a difference, keeping Rhiann for almost the last Singer to add their god's nature to the web. His work showed even something more. His flaws, the lack of the foot that sometimes caused him trouble, were actually necessary. Where everyone else was whole, because of the nature Ollahm himself had, Rhiann had to be flawed, had to be weakened, because weakness was a part of the nature of the world as much as strength was. In some ways, almost scarily, Hela realized that Rhiann's song took up where her own had left off, showing how to overcome destruction, how to build and become more than you were before.

It seemed that the world faded into darkness as Kialor wove in Lady Night's control to the web. In some ways, his was the most important. He would be combining the web with the Tapestry, bringing fate to rule over all of the world, not only the peoples that the gods had known from the beginning. He had the hardest job, because he must now not only channel his Goddess' nature, but he had to bind it, carefully combine it with the Tapestry and the Web, connect the two, and then merge them. He would be overflowing with energy, yet at the same time, he had to be working that energy, directing it, making this entire maelstrom work. It was a difficult job, and, even with the pain she'd experienced from Vythen's nature, Hela did not envy him. She knew that he would be nearly overborne by what he must do, but that he also wouldn't dare fail. It was not in his nature to fail, even as it was not in the nature of their aunt, Selah, to fail. Most of Lady Night's servants were like that, finding some way, no matter what was happening, to make things work out 'right'. Though their notions of right might be different from that of anyone else.

The darkness persisted longer than the weaving of any other set of energy. It was clearly a struggle for Kialor to keep functioning. And yet, that awareness became brighter, the longer it went on. It had help, though Hela couldn't imagine where that help had come from. Something was giving them all strength, giving them all the means to continue through the exhaustion of this Music. She didn't know what it was, or who it might be. She just knew that it was happening.

Then, almost at once, everything seemed to spring into focus. The need to continue the music vanished, much as if it had never been. Hela found her voice dying in her throat, even as the rest of the room fell silent. She opened her eyes, not to find a maelstrom of light and sound and madness, but a stone room, with circles carved into the floor, and her companions. And, beyond them, a ring of beings that seemed to glow, seemed not quite solid. They were linked, too many for her to count, each holding hands around the outside of the final ring. They said nothing, merely let go of those hands, even as Hela began to sink to the floor, trying to recover what she'd spent.

Chapter 13

Maskar felt completely drained as silence fell over the chamber. Part of that was being underground. He couldn't regain his energy here, and may have to be carried out into the sunlight, just to manage what he needed to for his health. Doubtless all of the others here were exhausted too, because a working like this took everything you had and then some. He'd been prepared for it. He was fairly certain that no one else, save perhaps Dastyl and Redel, had experienced anything this difficult.

He was barely able to open his eyes when he felt arms around him, catching him as his legs began to buckle. *It wasn't fai*r, he thought vaguely, *I've done this before. I shouldn't be this weak.* But the arms that held him weren't those of any of his companions, not even Evanira's. Instead, he found his eyes focusing on a face he had never wanted to see again, one that, for all Maskar's own hatred, seemed completely serene and gentle. And he had no strength to even begin to protest what was being done to him.

Almost instantly, the scene changed, without the lurch that Maskar had had when Grandmother or Grandfather managed the stepping between places. He found himself being laid down on the ground under the morning sun, finding that, wherever he was, it was soft here, and warm. Moments later, a flask of some form of liquid was being brought to his lips. If he had had any strength, he would have tried to refuse it, considering its source. But he couldn't do so. In fact, his body started greedily sipping the liquid, almost like it were drawing in liquid sunlight, something that would strengthen him on multiple levels. It was given in silence, as if any sound at all might break him. Perhaps that was fairly close to being true.

Almost as suddenly, several minutes later, while Maskar was merely drinking in the light that fell upon him, the celestial spoke. "Whether you wished it or not, Son, you did ask for aid. That aid was sent, turning away the power of your enemy, and coming to give succor to those who had succeeded where there was great chance of failure. I know that you hate still, that you might do so forever, but I was willing to bear that, so that none of our kin among the Heavens would have to endure your anger. That anger is unjust, whether you believe it or not, so I take it only upon myself, not letting any other feel that rage. In this, I allow you to strike, even as another did, long ago. Perhaps you learned enough from that that it is no longer such a need in you."

Maskar licked his lips, tried to draw moisture into his mouth, because he'd spent so much in the Song. Then, with halting words, he addressed the celestial who had both made sure he lived, and had chosen to allow him to exist in torment for a time. He hardly knew what he was saying, only knew that something had to be said.

"It is not what Kelu showed me that restrains my hand and mind today, nor is it the lack of energy that will only be filled by rest and light. It's something entirely different. I don't like you. I'm fairly certain I could never love you, not like Mother did. I don't know even if she understands what I wrote her, long ago. She never mentioned it in any letter she sent to Virea or myself. But my concern for someone else made me think, made me consider what I know, and what I thought I knew."

"Is that an overture for peace, Son?" Vehl's voice seemed hesitant, hopeful. It sounded like what Maskar would say now might be the most important things he'd ever said. The former thief wasn't sure he wanted to even consider that, not yet. Just as Vishti had not wanted to consider what was said about her mother's motives. It was easier to hate, to refuse any contact with the celestials. But, as Vehl had said, Maskar had in fact been the one to originate the idea of this Great Music, and, very clearly, he had asked for help to pull it off.

"It's an acknowledgement of situation, nothing more than that. I had to listen to someone explain their betrayal of someone they loved dearly. I didn't hear what came after, the meeting between Redel and Vishti's mother, but I don't think I need to hear that to realize something. Grandmother speaks sometimes about how every story has words that are not written down, things that exist outside of the teller's view, things that they cannot even begin to comprehend, but which direct their actions regardless. Seeing the two of them, I had to witness, very closely, how such stories can be very different, yet regard the same thing. I spoke with Vishti, afterward, pointed out that our viewpoint has a lot to do with what we take from a situation. Those words were for myself, just as much as they were for her."

The celestial was close, kneeling, even, just out of reach, if Maskar had the strength to move his arms enough to reach. Vehl lowered his head, almost out of Maskar's vision, his expression unreadable. But Maskar didn't need to see it to understand. It was a cusp, a place of decision, and Vehl knew that he could not rush Maskar, could not even try to direct him. To do so would bring failure to the hopes that the celestial had.

Trying to remember what he'd picked up from Vishti's conversation with Sihan'el, after the truth had been revealed, Maskar decided to attempt the same tactic, because it might be the only thing that could help him make the decision. "What was it," he carefully avoided calling Vehl Father, "that led you to decide that you would not interfere, once you knew where I was? What truth are you keeping from me about my own situation? I need to have those answers, before I can come to any real decision."

It was as if the sun had become much brighter, more nurturing, though Maskar couldn't understand it. Vehl moved slightly closer, where he could be seen, and where his fingers could trace the veins in Maskar's wrist, something that had always been easy to do, considering Maskar's extremely pale complexion.

"Son, have you not wondered why it is that you, specifically, seem immune to divinatory magics? Surely your grandparents have mentioned this to you. They've both tried to use them, and failed. They found something that even their Lady cannot pierce. And, indeed, it was to that Lady that I first came, when you were taken, looking for answers."

"They don't know why. They just know that such things fail, even blood divination. They can find Brehl with my blood, but not me, even with their own. It's like I'm invisible somehow."

"That is largely the truth, Son. You were shielded, veiled, by the only beings who can hide a mortal from the gods. The only time the gods themselves can perceive you, or any within the Heavens do so, is when you are involved in something else they are doing. They can only find you through another. The way your predicament was found, back in the warehouse that still haunts you, was because of threats to others. One of those watching, serving, realized the nature of that threat, and arranged for the best person available to be sent, Pharel, who serves Jirel. They couldn't tell where you were, only knew that you were somewhere there. They set free the tiger, convinced her to fight, to hunt and kill your captors. In that, they did the best thing they could do, and we realized that, by watching her, we could be aware of what happened to you, mostly, not entirely."

"You're saying that the faedh did this, made me unseeable to your magics?"

"They have their reasons, though I surmise that I might now know some of them. Even the words that you gave to the girl are important here. There were things you had to see, things you had to know, in order to even begin to help others. The faedh saw your potential, your strength. They knew that that strength had to be tempered with pain, loss, and fear, in order to give you the compassion you needed to become that hero that was necessary. Without your pain, so many others would have suffered and died, others who are now free, now safe from such depredations. Your compassion also allowed you to temper your gifts, even as our blessing, our power over you, taught you what it was like to be helpless, and to desire no such power over others. The faedh doubtless knew what we were doing with our blessings. They knew them as soon as they were laid, perhaps before. They decided that you would serve the needs of the world better with such helplessness. In the end, no matter how much pain you yourself bore, what you did was more important. What you did today no less so than what you'd done in Toyurasi, more than thirty years ago now. Are you going to turn your anger toward them, when you know you can only see part of what they are viewing, the need that they must solve?"

Maskar winced. He had definitely earned that rebuke, though it was almost as gentle as one from Uncle Rhiann. Indeed, there was too much in common between Vehl and Uncle Rhiann. It made the issue confusing, made him want to fight less. And, honestly, Uncle Rhiann would not want him to fight here. He would remind Maskar of the forgiveness Maskar himself had received from others, others who he'd hurt badly over the years, and ask if the denizens of the Heavens, and the spirits of the earth, were any less worthy of such forgiveness. And Maskar knew full well that he could never really argue with his uncle. Rhiann would never speak harshly with him, but his disappointment was something that Maskar simply could not face.

"I can't say that I appreciate what they did, what you did, but I think that I understand a few things now. You didn't answer everything, but I'm not sure you're allowed to. No matter how much I hurt when I think of what happened, what I'd endured, I have to acknowledge that perhaps it wasn't as bad as it could have been. I did survive, became a lot stronger than I ever really guessed. And I've used that strength to make sure that others don't have to suffer that."

Vehl leaned forward, placing a hand on Maskar's chest, softly, gently. It felt like some of the energy that Maskar had spent in the music was restored, almost instantly. Maskar decided that he'd try to earn his Uncle's approval in at least one way. He reached up and clasped the arm that hand was attached to, a firm clasp, not angry now. Then he nodded. "Let the war between us be over, Father. I can't say that this pain will ever go away, but I won't face life with the instinct of attacking you or the other denizens of the Heavens, not without good reason."

A light seemed to fill Vehl's eyes, eyes that matched the Ollahmic blue clothing he wore. "That is a gift I didn't expect from you. But I should return you to your kin. You have sufficient strength for now." There was another instantaneous transition, and Maskar found himself indoors again, and quickly the celestial was gone, without another word.

Chapter 14

Sihan'el had taken a moment, after most of the people involved in the direct song had collapsed, to make sure that Vishti was recovering, before he went to check on Hela. Even in the midst of the chaos of the music, the effort he was putting into keeping Vishti functional, he had heard the tones of absolute pain in Hela's voice. There was little he could do for either, but he needed to make sure that both were recovering before he'd take any rest for himself. His part had been small. Theirs had clearly been nearly overwhelming. And, while he didn't feel any different, he imagined that the participants might have different views of it.

Kialor was still on his hands and knees, and had crawled in Vishti's direction. Sihan'el had little fear that the healer would spend his last energy, if necessary, to get Vishti through what had just happened. And, with these strange glowing people present, he doubted that it would get to that kind of danger. They hadn't moved forward, save for the one that had grabbed Maskar so quickly and vanished, but whoever they were, they had been involved in what had happened. Sihan'el liked to consider that they were allies, but he couldn't be certain, not yet.

Father was likewise still mobile, though that barely. His soulsword might be feeding him energy, even if he wasn't in direct physical contact with it. Sihan'el had heard, from the other Sacred Sword, that the swords do provide energy when a knight needs help or healing. Father's connection with the relic was through his tah'nel, so physical contact might actually not be necessary in this case.

Hela was in a heap, which couldn't be comfortable, since she was still wearing armor. Sihan'el moved to straighten her out, pulling that golden hair from her face, rubbing at the sweat that seemed to have dried on her from the experience. She was hardly coherent, and he knew that what little he could do would be little help. He wasn't meant as help, especially not with that healing talent of hers, the ras'lah'tan. He was meant to be at her side when she awoke, trying to do more than keep the promises he'd made just a few nights back. No matter how poor others might consider his dedication, he did intend to make sure that she remained as comfortable as he could make her.

He didn't hear as one of the strange people came up. He only knew it when he could see the golden robes, the edges of the powerful wings that graced the back of this one. Sihan'el looked up, even as those wings spread, and the being knelt down beside Hela, placing one long-fingered hand on her chest. There were no words. Sihan'el knew that if this being meant her harm, there was not a thing he could do about it. He just wasn't strong enough. While he was mobile, he was not strong enough to fight, and knew that very well. He just had to trust that this being did not mean her any ill.

She stirred, eyes opening, widening for a moment, but no sound came from her mouth. The being produced a flask from seemingly nowhere, and tipped it to her lips. It splashed at first, then she was gulping the liquid down, so fast that it almost started her coughing. Her fingers splayed, then tightened, and she struggled to sit up as the flask was removed from her lips.

Then the being reached out to touch Sihan'el, something that almost made him jump back. The touch conveyed warmth, and strength. Sihan'el couldn't help but draw in a deep breath, just as if he were drawing in the energy that flowed from the being's hands. Hela looked at him, shook her head. She hadn't regained her voice, but she made it clear soundlessly that he should accept this. He waited until the hand was withdrawn, then inclined his head in thanks.

The being merely nodded, moved on to someone else. Whoever these beings were, they were clearly here to help. Nothing else made sense to him. He had no idea what they were, or who had sent them. All he really knew was that they had appeared from nowhere, and that their luminosity was not unlike that which Maskar had at times, a luminosity that had been shared by a woman in Sharlan as well, a woman whose back was graced with similar wings, only wings like opal, rather than like gold.

Hela coughed a bit, then managed to make a sound, not much of one, but at least a sound. It was a sign of recovery. After a moment, she formed words, though they were halting and faint. "You don't know, do you? That was one of the Risen One's celestials. That's the only thing he could have been. I'm sure that there are some from the other churches, too. I didn't expect to see them. I had no idea that they'd be sent to aid us. And I think they did more than the healing."

Sihan'el didn't even think about that. Instead, he reached out to pull Hela closer to him, sliding her across the floor so that she lay against his chest, propped up by the fact that he wasn't lying flat. "I heard the pain. I don't know what that was, but I couldn't help you. I have no means to do so. Vishti, well, she's different. It was bad, wasn't it?"

Hela winced, and readjusted herself. "It was my Lord's power. I'm not surprised. He reminded me, in the Song, that I had more ability to deal with it than anyone else in his service. Beyond being of the People, I have the ras'lah'tan, and that does make a difference. I could heal, was healing, at the time the power ran through me. And I couldn't let myself be any less than Rhiann was. He'd sung a device to power twice, while standing on a newly made false foot, only minutes after having had his cut off. To do less than he did…" She didn't complete the sentence.

Sihan'el pulled her head to his shoulder. "Don't try to do anything, Hela. You need rest. They took Maskar, one of those celestials as you called them. I don't know why, but I imagine he'll be back soon. His healing might be different, even though he wasn't at the heart of this. Just rest, try to regain your strength. I know we won't have much time, perhaps a day or so before we return to the Covert, and then, well, I think Father intends to have us marching to war as soon afterward as we can. So we must rest while we may."

She half-turned, snuggling herself against him. It was almost like it had been on their wedding night, now only a few days past. What he'd done to her, before Father and Ranor showed up, had left her utterly drained. In a way, he liked that. It was a power he never expected to have. And to have her actually seeming to want nothing but to drink in his presence, that felt comfortable, right. It made him wonder more at what his father knew. There had to be more to Redel's calmly phrased statements than just the fact that there had been no hint of a law broken. Whatever it was, he imagined Hela knew, though she too had not expected him to be so completely serene about finding them in that state. Not a single rebuke, or even the hint of one.

Even as he sat there, one arm bracing them up, one wrapped around her to keep her from slipping from her position, he heard an awkward and heavy step. He half expected to see Father standing over him, but it was someone else entirely, his cousin Rhiann, the Singer who had been the next to the last of the god-touched to give up that power.

He didn't kneel. That made since, because his foot would have given him too much trouble. Instead, he merely stood there a long moment watching them, a wry smile on his face. "I had had doubts before, despite Ranor's insistence on what he'd seen. I think I see it too, now."

Sihan'el moved slightly, still not letting go of Hela, but moving to a more upright position. "Doubts on what?" His tone was slightly irritated, even though he'd discovered quickly enough that he liked this priest, almost against his will, even.

Rhiann tilted his head, "I had doubts that there was anything more to this than business. Not that that always works out poorly. I've seen what happened to your father, almost terrified at first of the bride he'd won. Though Yossa says that Ael'yn can be difficult to deal with, I think Redel has found her less so. And if you can tame my uncle's wild daughter, perhaps in time even he will see that this is to all of our benefits. You only barely checked to make sure that aid was going to Vishti. You have not checked on your other sister. Yet you sit here, with Hela curled against you as if there was no other place to be in the world. There is much more to what I see than can easily be explained."

Sihan'el looked up, glancing around the chamber to see if he could find Sai'velk. Yes, he had forgotten about her entirely, focused only on the sister he knew well and the wife he had claimed for himself. And that claim was almost in the same way that she said her sister had been claimed, and her mother. He wasn't sure what to make of that yet, but he realized that it did indeed feel different, coming to Hela, trying to succor her without any hope of doing so.

Rhiann seemed to know what he was thinking, or at least where his eyes had gone. The priest nodded and smiled. "I still will say nothing to her father, or our grandfather. It is best that you present that. But, when the time comes, if you need any voices to calm their fears, mine will be among them. And both of them listen to me, so perhaps that will make it easier."

"Thank you," Sihan'el managed, still awkward with the customs of the west. Then he looked back down at Hela, stroked back her hair, and drunk in her scent. This actually felt good, much to his surprise. He needed little else.

Chapter 15

Kialor held Vishti as she recovered, her strength repaired by the celestial. His own recovery might be slower, not because of a lack of physical strength, but because his awareness had changed so completely during this ritual. They had succeeded. There was no doubt about that, though he wasn't sure how they'd gotten past the sheer pain that Hela was going through when it had become her time to transfer the divine energy. Kialor could barely touch it. Only his determination to get things done allowed him to weave those threads into the web he was holding, that Vishti was powering in her own way. He would have tried to check on Hela, but he'd seen Sihan'el move there, and, even after Vishti was aware, her body pressed up against his, he didn't think it a good idea to move. Sihan'el might not be a healer, but Hela had ras'lah'tan. She would recover, though it might take her longer than she expected.

Vishti was perhaps as drained as he was, not physically, because the celestials had restored their physical selves to near perfection, but of mental and spiritual capacity, yes, she'd been drained. They had both been the ones to handle the hard parts of this task. She had held the magic together, while he'd been doing all of the weaving, in addition to the channeling of his Goddess that Kialor had done. Which is why no one had come to even suggest that they move from where they lay.

Movement caught Kialor's eye, and he could see Redel stoop to help Sai'velk to her feet. The colors that had been so vivid in her before were drained, likely because of so much phoenix fire burning through her during the ritual. There was a story, still told among the family, of how one of the family matriarchs had done something similar. Lady Mialar had burnt herself out of magic completely, a situation that had lasted years. In that, her hair, which Grandfather Arandel described as brightly golden, and the eyes that burned with her divine father's phoenix fire, had both dulled, becoming little more than mortal, though she could not die, not in truth. Kialor expected that much of the same happened when Sai'velk channeled that power. It wasn't quite as much, and not the same, but it did burn her internally, and she would be weak for a time.

Vishti moved, murmuring incoherently. He stroked her hair, then rubbed on her cheeks, where the marks that showed what she'd been through seemed very faded. Perhaps the celestial's healing had done more than intended. It was a pity, really, because it had added a depth of character to Vishti that he'd grown to love. And, as he thought that, he realized that that was true. It was something he loved, with a tenderness and desire. His body probably wasn't capable of acting on that desire. His mind certainly wasn't, at this stage, but he knew it was there. He felt a sudden contentment, and tightened his arm around her. "Peace, Vishti. We did it. Just relax for now."

There were footsteps, and he could see Redel walking carefully over to him, almost gingerly, in fact. He had been one of the few to remain on their feet as silence had fallen. But it was clear that he too had been drained by this. Perhaps he was only sustained by SkySong. At his side was Sai'velk, who looked sadly at the way Vishti was lying against Kialor's side.

Kialor looked up, "It worked, Father, Sister. I can see how the two have merged, the web and the Tapestry. It means that we probably won't have time, though I can do little now, and Vishti probably less."

Redel nodded, dropping to a knee. "We need to get the two of you to where you can rest. The Scholars have a place for us, and Maskar's already been taken. I don't know why it was as hard as it was on him, but I imagine there's a reason. He's usually stronger for such things. Can you at least walk, Kialor? If I need to, I can carry Vishti. It's not far, thankfully. I just don't think she'll trust one of the Scholars if they try."

Kialor nudged Vishti, trying to focus on bringing her mind to the fore. "Vishti, we need to go to rest. Your father offered to carry you. I'm pretty sure I can't. Not yet."

She opened her eyes, seeming to focus on the two people standing near her. "You won't leave me?"

"Of course not. I'm going to need as much rest as you do, Vishti. I will only be a step or two away." He helped roll her into a position that Redel could take Vishti, though it would doubtless be difficult for him. Then, with that burden off of his side, he grimaced and forced his limbs back into motion, managing to unsteadily make it to his feet. To his surprise, Sai'velk steadied him, offering him an arm to lean on. He didn't like having to lean on anyone, but there really wasn't much of a choice. His sense of direction seemed fogged, where it shouldn't normally do that ever, and his balance was far from adequate. He needed the help, no matter how he felt about it.

Redel seemed to have some of the same problem, but again, there were the advantages of the soulsword at his back. He spoke softly with the nearest Scholar, then moved down one of the halls, deeper into the keep. Kialor followed, using Sai'velk's strength to steady him. She'd had a lesser part in this, and seemed to have regained more of her nature. Perhaps it was simply that she hadn't had to spend any energy afterward, like he had with Vishti. No matter how drained he had been, he knew that he'd had to stabilize his wife as soon as he could get to her. Managed that much even before the celestials had gotten to them.

It was a short passage, then a room with real beds. Redel stood for a moment while Kialor pulled back the blankets, then laid her on the bed itself, finishing with pulling off her boots. Kialor almost stumbled as he moved to lay down himself. He knew that Father and Sai'velk would be lying down soon, and probably the rest of the group too. Almost to his surprise, Kialor realized that he knew, without looking, where every person in here was. It was easier than his prior attempts to see people's life threads. He could see them all, naturally, fully. And could see how the crux had happened, the tying of all of the threads only perhaps a half candlemark past.

Sai'velk moved to look down at Vishti, not ready to lie down herself yet. Then, with a gentle touch, she rubbed at those scars. There was sorrow in those golden eyes, sorrow and weariness. "She took on too much," the priestess murmured. "Even with our brother's help, it was almost too much for her. She needs more time, and we have little enough of that left to us."

Kialor turned a bit, wrapping an arm around Vishti, then lifting her head enough that he could get it over his other arm. "She's stronger than she looks, Sai'velk. She's possibly stronger than anyone guesses. I've seen that, in how she's dealt with certain shocks. I'm sure she'll survive this, though it will be hard on her."

The priestess nodded, pulling the blankets up and over Kialor and Vishti. "I don't know if I could have stood what she'd gone through. The pain, hatred, and killing. I've never been to the point of doing that, though, once, I thought I was. The Risen One must have been touching my soul even then, because he kept me from despair. I think she's known a lot of despair."

Vishti stirred, "Maskar said that what I went through was so that I could do good for others. I want to believe that. I want to think that it wasn't for nothing. But I can't be certain, not yet. I don't even know if it gave me the strength for this, what we just did."

Kialor pressed her against him, drinking in the feeling he had. "Vishti, I think you've already done so much for us, for me, even. I know you don't understand this, but I can say I'm happier, now that I have more of a purpose. I think it is like Grandfather Caldor and Hlasa, or even, in a lesser way, with Lilith. He needs to be needed. I think I did too. And I've found out that my words from a few nights ago are truer than I thought."

She half turned to look at him, "Kialor?"

He took his arm that was on top of her and went to touch her on the lips, "I realized that this is love. Nothing short of that could have gotten me moving after the Music ended. I had to get to you. I wasn't going to let anything stop me."

Sai'velk smiled, nodding, "He did not give up, even when I could barely hold my head off the ground, he was crawling to you, forcing himself to make each movement. If that is love, I wish to someday find someone like that to show me its nature. I had once thought I had desire, for the golden ghost who rescued me, but I don't think it was anything like this. Perhaps later, I will meet him again, as I have been told that he often comes among the people at your home."

Kialor acknowledged the statement. "I've met him. So has Sihan'el, apparently. Xereff was one of those who went with Maskar to get Sihan'el from where he was hiding. He's a good man, though I know nothing of where his intentions lie. I'm not sure he's been open with them, at least not publicly."

Sai'velk bent over, placing a kiss on Vishti's forehead. That might have been a bad idea, except that Vishti wasn't likely to move, this time. She merely shivered, and pressed closer to Kialor. Then Sai'velk half-bowed, and moved away, likely to her own rest.

Chapter 16

No one had arrived yet to take back the two priests from Sharlan, but that was expected shortly. In the meantime, everyone took time to recover from the strains of the Great Music. The fact that the gods now had a more direct way to sense the kee-ali-dahlri made a difference, perhaps a big one. Each of the priests realized that their awareness was heightened, more easily accessed than it had been. The same went for the one Chosen among the group, Redel, who found that there was perhaps a little less resistance in his soul toward the faith that he knew was far from perfect. Perhaps that had been a good part of what his trouble had been, he acknowledged. Not only had his background made him resistant to it, but there had been something in his very blood that had made it more difficult.

Vishti sat down with her family, almost for the first time acknowledging that that was true of all of them. Dastyl had backed away, and none of the other Scholars were interfering, so it was only those of Calasti lineage present in the dining area where everyone had gathered. She could see her cousin Rhiann shifting uneasily on the bench that he needed just to sit down properly. She knew that these days had been hard on him, not only missing his wife and daughter, but also simply with the physical limitations of his leg. She could see Father, leaning against the wall, sense the restlessness in him. It was a restlessness that infected most of the company. There was little that could be done about it.

Vishti looked at Kialor, tried to smile for his sake. "You look like you're more afraid of what you've done than what we will be doing."

He laughed, "I think that might be it. I didn't set out to be anything more than a potter, and maybe a healer on occasion. Now, well, I'm not so sure that I will ever be able to go back to that. Too many things have changed."

Ranor spoke up, from only a few feet away. "If only we could have Uncle Kelu to talk to you. He might have some advice for that, considering how greatly things changed for him, and most of it because of his own actions."

Kialor shook his head, "He's gone for rebirth, from what Vehlan said. It's strange that it happened when it did, though I'm certain there was a reason, perhaps a very good reason. But yes, he would have given me good advice, I think. I just wish I knew what to do with the restlessness of my soul."

Hela, much to Vishti's surprise, wiped a tear from her face. She glanced over at Sihan'el next to her and made a faint laugh, though to what, Vishti didn't even guess. Then her words came, wistful, with a touch of pain. "I think he would have been very amused to see me now. Perhaps my sister would be too, though she won't know, not for a while, what's happened. It's strange. Everyone thought that I would want someone I could dominate, someone I could use for my advantages. That's not how things turned out at all. Kelu might have known. If he did, he kept it quiet. The thing was, back in Sharlan, there was no one who dared challenge me, to show me that I didn't have to command to be comfortable. Uhbara would understand, even if I can't hope for Father to."

From his place, Rhiann nodded, "You needed to get to a place where you could let go, indeed, likely be forced to let go, before you could find peace. That alone might make things different when you do get home, should you succeed in the battles to come. No, Uncle Maran wouldn't understand, but you'll find allies in both your mother and sister, I think."

Hela shrugged, "While I know that it was earned other ways, one of the things I remember most about Kelu is that, aside from Father for a long time, no one really had a lack of respect for him. And I know that Father was not one to try to put Kelu in his place, really ever. I doubt anyone could have actually defied him."

From the corner, one voice disagreed. "You can verify this with Evanira, and, later, my Grandfather, but there is someone that Kelu had a very hard time winning over. Honestly, that may have been one of my worst mistakes, though I didn't understand it at the time. I only saw something that reminded me of my past, of my fears. He tried to guide me gently, then, when I refused and became defensive, tried command. Neither worked. I'm still not sure why it was that I managed to walk away from that. With his pride, it had to be hard not to strike back, not after I'd just outright refused to obey him, then deliberately turned my back on him and walked away. I knew what I was doing. I wanted, at that time, for him to strike back. It would have been easier. He didn't. I don't think I'll ever know why."

Rhiann nodded to Maskar. "He didn't because he knew, though he did not know why, that you were at that spot. He knew that you were stressed to the breaking point by something, and that you would not have bent if he'd applied pressure or power. You would have broken. You would have resisted till death, at that point. It's not the only time you've gotten there, either. You do have a very bad habit of trying to force the powerful to strike you."

Maskar shrugged, nodded. "Yes, I know that. I also know that, for whatever reason, those with power don't exert it when I get to that point. Not many would have dared insulting a god to his face. It still amazes me that not only did he not strike me down, but he continued to offer us help. I didn't deserve that mercy, especially not then."

Sai'velk swayed suddenly from where she stood, her eyes wide and focused on Maskar. Vishti didn't understand the fear, partly because she really didn't know anything about the gods, beyond what she'd experienced through the Music. And that was different. She only held the power. All else was just a brush against her mind. "You defied a god? And spoke with him directly at the time?"

Rhiann lifted a hand, trying to stop this before it went in the wrong direction. "Sai'velk, you were told that things are different where we live. Well, it's mostly different for us. Our children, Maskar's son Brehl and my daughter Yossa, had been taken. It was a part of what made this situation here happen, because it allowed the knowledge and weapons from long ago to be returned to this world. Because of how they were taken, and where, a place that was both a part of and separate from our world, the gods themselves became involved. My daughter, Yossa, has a half-brother, Zenir. He is Vythen's own son, though purely mortal because of how he'd been conceived. Vythen felt he owed a debt to Iltres, Zenir's and Yossa's mother. So, when the gods received word from one of the demi-divine, Grandmother Mialar, Vythen himself came to bring us word, to bring us tools we could use. I'm sorry to say that Maskar treated him poorly, despite the help offered. Perhaps in time, he will learn that such anger is unnecessary."

Maskar coughed, "I think I already have. The celestial who came for me, gave me exactly what I needed after that working, was my father. I've spoken with him, found out more than I expected to. As a result, I've offered peace, though I still don't feel that I can hold any feelings for him. There's too much pain, too much anger still hiding. I might not act out my anger. I learned that lesson all too quickly after having my geas removed. That doesn't mean that the anger isn't there, eating away at me. It seems to have become a little less, and I think, in time, I might be grateful for that, but it will take time. We just have to make sure that we all have the kind of time to come to terms with our own changes. That's not guaranteed yet."

Vishti was surprised to hear the chagrin in Maskar's voice. Always before, even when he was helping her, he seemed to have a lot more pride, a lot more power. Today, well, he sounded weak, ashamed of himself. And yet, there was also a sense of relief in his voice, if she was listening to it properly.

Rhiann, on the other hand, positively beamed. "I imagine that such an offer took him by surprise. Grandfather has spoken with him, heard the pain in his voice when he spoke of how he'd alienated you. I think, more than anything else, Vehl is a father in this. He wants to be able to show his love, and has been stymied by both of his children. Maybe, if you've found a possible path to peace, there is hope for Virea, too. That would be something of a miracle, I think, that the two of you find a way to divest yourselves of your anger and resentment."

Vishti leaned against Kialor and looked around. "Perhaps what we have done has done more than we thought? Perhaps now there is a chance of peace, even with our enemy?"

Kialor wrapped his arm around her. "Vishti, you're the one who had that vision, the one that had you choosing between killing and healing our enemy. I don't know how we could heal her. If there's a path like that, it belongs in your hands, perhaps already in your mind. I can't think of anything that could release a mind trapped in that much pain. It was more than you bore, and remember, there is much that still needs healing in you. The only possible way I can think of for offering her peace would take away what she is, in a way. Losing her past might heal her, but I'm not sure that's possible."

Vishti felt something stirring within her, but it offered no immediate answer. "I will think on that. Perhaps I will have to hear from each of you, on the nature of your souls' wounds, to find something that could offer peace, rather than destruction. Maskar has told me that death should not be the solution sought for much of anything. If there is a way to bring healing, that would be better, even with what was done to me."

Rhiann reached out, clasped one of Vishti's hands in his. "Cousin, if you, who were most damaged by her ill, can say that, perhaps there is hope. Not many can look for that. And I believe that I will enjoy time spent getting to know you better, once this is done."

It wasn't much, but it was a promise, in a way, of a better time. Vishti thought that that might be what she wanted, more than anything else.

Chapter 17

Hela, despite their success at the Great Music, which had given her a lot stronger connection with the Dread Lord, felt a certain wariness as they rode back toward the Rhi'na'n covert. She couldn't exactly put her finger on what had changed, but knew that their enemy was up to something, perhaps something that they didn't expect at all. There was a nagging sense that the Great Mother was aware of them, perhaps had even identified who they were. Whether that was true or not, she didn't know. She did know that the feeling did not go away, despite their steady progress toward what had been safety, and likely would be again. They just had to set in motion plans that could defeat the Mayisna, one way or another.

Sai'velk was with them, despite her unfamiliarity with the outside world in recent decades. The priestess only said that they would probably need another healer, and that was something she had at least some power with. Her phoenix fire would also be useful in open combat, should that be needed. However, the Scholars declined to leave their fortress at this time, saying that there were other preparations they would make, and that they had to prepare for even more madness that would likely come from the Great Mother being stymied like this.

If what Maskar said was true, the constructs would have lost their power shortly after the Great Music ended. And would have been worthless before that, due to the nature of the changes in life-force that had happened accordingly. With all of the kee-ali-dahlri, and potentially both the Sa'eh and their counterparts, being related by blood to the kee-ali-dahlri, altered somewhat by the inclusion of the gods' power in their nature, there was enough of a difference in nature to make things both easier and harder. It should make them only have to fight flesh and blood enemies, but what else might happen was still a mystery.

She could hear the rest of the company, most notably Sihan'el who rode beside her, and could feel his tension. Last night he'd had nightmares. He wouldn't talk about them, but she'd been at his side as he thrashed in the bedding. When she'd queried about their nature, he only told her that they were related to some memories. She knew that he'd been present at one of the attacks on a Rhi'na'n covert. He had also gone looking through others, trying to find those he knew and cared about. At least one of those closest to him was dead. It could well be that his nightmares dwelt upon that, which would be enough to stress anyone out.

She remembered how badly her brother hurt, not only losing his wife, but a son and his wife as well, only a few years apart. Khimel had died early, and Dareen hadn't wanted to continue after that. Hlasa, well, Hlasa had been Caldor's life for a long time. There was a great deal of time between her death and Lilith being brought to him, where there were doubts as to how strong Caldor was, emotionally. He had seemed so fragile, despite being built like Father. If Sihan'el had reason to become that fragile, well, it wasn't a good situation.

Hela looked over to Sihan'el, trying to be gentler, especially since she knew that she needed to make some form of bond that would make keeping her oath easier. "Are you ready to tell me what was so painful last night? I know it hurt, a lot, but your pulling away didn't help with it. If you can't talk to me, and I'd understand if that's the case, you should talk to someone, perhaps Kialor, or your father? We might be heading into battle. Anything that disrupts your focus is going to make it harder to keep the team alive. And that is our intent."

He glanced at her, and then away. "There are times, much like what Maskar was admitting to the other day, when I'm not sure I want to keep alive. I know what we need to do, but there's so much that I'm not ready to face, so much I'm not prepared to deal with. Last night proved that to me."

That didn't sound good at all. There was a deep ache to his voice, and a sense of pulling away, even so close after their marriage. It gave her an idea of what Vishti had gone through, right at the beginning, when Kialor couldn't face what he was dealing with. They had gotten past that first difficulty, but whether she could do so with Sihan'el was less certain.

"No one can help you find that peace if you're not willing to open up. I am your wife now, and you agreed to that willingly, even started the process with your father, finding the agreements that would make this work. I'm not an enemy, as you should know. But you're still largely closed off to me. I wish I knew what to do better to fix that."

His voice was almost a growl. "You probably don't want to know what I dreamed. Especially with that bond in place. Not now that you have a right to take it as betrayal."

So, he'd dreamed of a former lover? And he expected such dreams to merely go away, simply because of the bond of earth? She knew that they wouldn't. There was no way to make them do so. His contact with other women was a part of his past, just as her former lovers were a part of hers. "I knew of your experience long before I took those oaths, Sihan'el. I don't expect you to forget them, or for them not to crop up in your mind now and again. That's just something I have to accept. Neither of us claimed innocence, and we both have pasts, good and bad, that will crop up from time to time. I agreed to accept any children you might have fathered. That meant that I understand where you're coming from. Do you have any doubts that I'll forgive such a dream?"

He winced, "That's not all of it, though I wasn't so sure that you'd forgive that, not now that you've claimed me like this." So, he, like his father, still had that inherent sense that because they were both male, even with the dominance that each could, and did, assert, they were still largely property of their wives. Something that would probably shock Father even more than her marriage itself would. "I saw my son's mother, but she wasn't whole. There were tears in the skin, and a smell of rot, but she moved, lumbered for me, and, in that state of decay, tried to do things that would disgust anyone. You expect me to feel comfortable with anything touching me after that?"

"You saw her as if she were dead? Or perhaps of the Dead? A physical corpse made a mockery of life? That would be disturbing, though I think it was likely just a nightmare made from stress. I would think that even among your people, it is considered an abomination to abuse a corpse. I don't know what method you use for disposing of them, but I do expect that there is respect for them."

"From what I gather, especially from my dealings with the Elder Sisters, most of our people do respect the dead. When my brother fell, and I found his corpse, I built a cairn, to protect the corpse from beasts that might come. I built that with my own two hands, feeling that I needed to do something to honor Vedask. I wonder, sometimes, if his spirit is out there, trying to convey something to me. I wonder if he thinks I'd betrayed him, somehow, by not being there when the attack hit. The same with Vashk and his mother. I don't have much hope of either being alive, but I need to hope for something, and the most I can is that Vashk was protected, somewhere, by someone. I can't be certain, but that's where my hopes lie."

Hela wished that she could be more of a comfort to Sihan'el right now. The gods knew that he'd done so much, when the Music ended, forcing his way to her and just holding her when her mind and body were awash with the memory of the pain she'd been in. She'd been strong enough. Vythen had been right. Of all of his servants, she was the only one with ras'lah'tan. She could survive what would likely kill a normal priest or Fang. And yet, Sihan'el had not mocked her weakness after the song had ended. He'd merely gotten to her and held her, almost like he were feeding her what strength he had left. It had been a blessing she hadn't expected, but now decided she craved. As he had gone beyond what he'd promised, she felt the need to do the same. It was something that Rhiann had been surprised by, though he only supported what he saw there.

"Sihan'el, tonight, at camp, maybe I should help you to relax more. Not necessarily what we have been doing, but perhaps something different. I might not be the best at such things, but would a massage help, something to take your mind off of what you've lost these past moons? I wish we had something more, something to distract us, but I doubt that they have anything of that sort among the Rhi'na'n."

There was a hint of a laugh, "Depending on what sorts of things you're looking for to distract, there may well be. We've got a lot of herb lore, and some things are made often, and used in cases like this, even. When someone is heartsick, and it does happen, a lot, when you're fighting the Great Mother, they sometimes need something to take their minds off of their troubles. A dose like that, then perhaps a night just curled up next to you, might be pleasant enough. It might let me focus later on what we need to do."

Hela smiled, "I hadn't guessed that there would be something like that, though I imagine you know the camp better than I do. It sounds enjoyable. And maybe we'll break through some of those barriers of yours while we're at it."

He snorted, "You're welcome to try, Hela. It's not like I don't belong to you now." But there was a hint of irony in his tone. It made the former bitterness he'd had with the idea a little more poignant.

Chapter 18

Camp had been nice. Hela had made it nicer, sharing a drink that allowed relaxation with him. And, just as she'd promised, much to his surprise, she'd worked on his muscles, shoulders, back, and even legs, to help loosen the knots that had been there for moons. He hadn't expected her to give him that kind of attention. Truth be told, he'd never been on the receiving end of it before. No Sister would have done it, and the Rhi'na'n still had many of the kril'dga prejudices. Hela, however, was outside of that, and, despite her pride, or perhaps because of it, she willingly placed herself in situations that the kril'dga would have found demeaning. First she allowed him to bind her, to overwhelm her with his desires, and then this. It was all a very new set of feelings for him, though he enjoyed it immensely.

He'd barely gotten food in him the next morning before his nose started picking up something strange. Kialor was nearby, had just reached over to kiss Vishti, something he'd begun doing fairly often now. He suddenly pulled away, eyes widening, and sprang to his feet. That was sufficient sign for alarm. The priest might not be trained to survive out here, but he did have amazing senses for danger.

Kialor pulled Vishti to her feet, then rang out warning calls in the Old Tongue, calls that carried over the distance clearly. "We're under attack. The enemy knows where we are!"

Sihan'el crossed the space between them, almost subconsciously calling for the elements, letting wind buffer him and flame flicker around his fingertips. "You're sure?"

"She's apparently been aware of us since the Music. Why she didn't do anything then, I don't know, but I caught a glimpse of her mind just now, in Vishti's. There's a chance she's spying through others, too, probably anyone who was a part of the Music who has an active tah'nel."

The camp was rousing, and Kialor looked at Vishti hard, "Get the horses. We don't have much time. I'll try to join you when I can, but I need to see this."

"I'm better at fighting, Kialor."

"You're better close in. I'm just there to look, to understand. And we need the horses ready. Hela is going to have to be at the front. Her power, Sihan'el's and Sai'velk's can all damage from a distance. That gives us more time. But we will need the horses. Hurry."

Vishti looked like she was going to argue some more, but Sihan'el shook his head. Then, moments later, Vishti was gone, running past tents and shelters, toward where the horses had been picketed. He just hoped she was fast enough at it. It was, largely, a new skill for her, though Kialor had been showing her how to handle them for a while now. And the horses wouldn't respond as well without an experienced rider controlling them. Hopefully they didn't panic. That would make a bad situation worse.

Sihan'el glanced at Kialor, then gestured around, "Near the entrance?"

"No, through the cleft. I don't know how they got there, but at least it offers us a better chance to slow them down. Hopefully your father will start the evacuation process. My senses tell me that we'll have to evacuate. I don't know what it is. It's not the constructs, certainly, but there's another danger, despite only a few of the kril'dga in that direction."

Almost on cue, Redel's voice rang through the encampment, giving orders for people to prepare to evacuate. He possibly already knew where the danger was. His sword might have told him, honestly. Sihan'el moved among the tents with Kialor right behind him, gathering a small following at the same time. Hela had caught up, an almost green light seeming to suffuse her, and right behind her was Sai'velk, though the latter seemed highly distressed. That was not unexpected. The priestess hadn't fought in years, if she'd done that at all. She might not have, seriously. Only been used for other purposes, purposes that might make it harder for her to do what she needed to do now.

Maskar seemed to appear out of nowhere, though how he could hide, Sihan'el never could figure out. With his coloration, not that far off from the celestials that had aided them at the Scholar's sanctuary, he shouldn't be able to vanish at all. *Then again,* Sihan'el remembered, *he has the same abilities to alter himself as I do. He could have been making himself less noticeable. That was well within his abilities.*

Even before they reached the narrow cleft that was used for bringing in food from outside, Sihan'el realized what was wrong. That smell was all too noticeable. It was a charnel scent, the odor of the grave. And it was the grave that was coming toward them, many half-eaten corpses, their features unreadable, lumbering through the gap, not at all fazed by the difficulty of the path or the traps that had been set to protect the camp. It was more than distressing. It was an abomination, even as Hela had described it before. No one should call up the Dead, but those had been called up, and, with a lurch of his stomach, Sihan'el could tell that these Dead were of the Rhi'na'n. His own allies and friends, thought lost, turned against him.

Suddenly Father was there, his soulsword held out in front of him, but only one handed. The other hand held a crystal, a set of bandoleers thrown over his armor that likely held a bunch more. It was a moment that Sihan'el could be proud to be Redel's son, if only because his father was proving himself to be exactly what Sihan'el had been afraid of at first, a powerful force of justice.

Redel's words came out quickly, even as a bolt of power struck one of the first corpses coming down the path. "They won't be easy to kill. We need energy, where possible. Mages and priests should use what they can to slow them, to damage the corpses so that they won't be able to move. Unfortunately, we've only got two resonant mages. Maskar and myself. None of the Rhi'na'n with that training survived prior attacks. Try to keep them at range. We might not be able to take them all down, but we can give the rest of the camp time to escape. We'll do a fighting retreat when we can. We just have to do our best."

Almost on cue, an explosion rocked a section of the path, with the earth seeming to rise up in anger at the defilement by the Dead. Sihan'el glanced around, then realized that Maskar was already Singing. He wasn't using his tah'nel, but actually Singing, and in a way that most weren't familiar with. Perhaps it was an ancient dah'ral skill. Whatever the source, Sihan'el was grateful for it, and for Maskar, no matter how difficult it had been for them to get along before.

Sihan'el saw the point his father had made, and began throwing fire at the nearest corpse. It wasn't the most powerful attack, but it could slow them down, and the fire could spread, especially if they got close to each other. That might be something to do. Maybe use a little wind to whip the flames, get them to damage as many of the corpses as they could. Fire might cause them to drop faster, at least make it impossible for them to fight. Burn the connections between the bones, and those will fall off.

Hela was chanting, sending sprays of what was likely acid at the enemies, while Sai'velk seemed to glow with a golden nimbus, throwing off bolts of golden fire against their foe. That did far better than Sihan'el's own fire, in fact. Something in the golden bolts damaged the corpses even more, causing them to shudder, and many of them to collapse. But they kept on coming.

Archers from the Rhi'na'n seemed to understand, and were launching flaming arrows into the pass, even as the people with damaging magic and mind-magic worked together to slow the advance. Sihan'el lost track of Kialor, but knew that the priest had little in the way of offensive magic. Perhaps he had other things that would work, instead. At the very least, Kialor was likely to coordinate what was going on with those who were trying to escape out of the main, normally guarded, entrance. That would be an important job, and anyone who could manage that would likely be an asset to the team. The only question was whether the Rhi'na'n would listen to him. He was very much male, and one who had said so little to their leaders over the time. If he was needing to communicate, he might have to pull Vishti from her job of readying the horses.

Almost from out of nowhere, a great cat, orange striped, moved onto the edge of the path where the Dead were still coming. Perhaps it could do little but slow down the enemies, but it could keep them from getting close to the casters while they retreated slowly back down toward where they could escape. That cat had to be Evanira. Sihan'el had seen it once before, when they'd fought the constructs at a prior camp. She hadn't gone that way during the fight in the keep, that he could remember, but he hadn't kept his eye on her. Instead, he'd been busy trying to get himself killed. That had not been a success, but mostly the fault for his survival rested in the form of the dah'ral Singer who was still causing explosions up and down the cleft, destroying many of the Dead that were coming at them, without need for attacks from others. The only problem was that the Dead kept coming.

Sihan'el could feel his strength beginning to fade, his ability to control that fire and wind lapsing from time to time. Thankfully, what he set on fire tended to stay on fire. That made it a little better. He just needed it to spread more. Then, quickly, he felt a tap on his shoulder. "Mount up. We've got most of the others out, and we're going to be covering them, where we can. I've got an idea that might slow them, for the moment. But we have to get out of the way." It was Kialor.

The archers and Rhi'na'n mages had already begun backing off, and the horses were here. Taking time between shots of power, each of the companions mounted up, except Evanira, who kept harrying those who were too close. Then Kialor shouted something to Evanira, and she jumped away. It was good that she did. The mountain walls on both sides of the cleft shifted, shattered, crumbled. The earth buckled, nearly unseating Sihan'el. Only the control that Kialor and Hela had kept those horses under control. There were still Dead on this side of what now closed the pass, but they wouldn't take much time over those, not now. Instead, it was time to flee. And the horses were already working to do it. Maskar didn't stop long enough to let Evanira shift back and mount up behind him, but moved on ahead. The cat merely followed, gracefully loping at his side.

Chapter 19

There were no words as the party hurried out of the main entrance of the covert, mostly them leaning very low over their horses' heads to get through the cavern that had concealed most of the camp. Kialor was amazed that his plan worked as well as it did, having Hela send a spark of destructive power into the cleft walls where there had been a few spikes drilled before for quick release, in case of a similar situation. She'd struck it just right, bringing the cleft down on itself, which gave them a bit of a head start, and possibly managed to kill at least one of the kril'dga that were commanding the corpsefolk. That would certainly slow them down. The mages handling the corpses would have to move around the mountain to find the Rhi'na'n and his own party, which gave them time to hide. Though Kialor himself wasn't sure how much hiding would help. Corpsefolk's only limitation really was that they needed to either be given set commands, or had to be handled by a mage. So there wouldn't be much delay in trying to find where the Rhi'na'n went.

He could tell that most of his people were exhausted, already. Hardly out of bed and having had to spend a great deal of energy to fend off an enemy force. And there was no hope of rest in the near future, and little hope of being able to hide for very long. They had some supplies, because Vishti had grabbed them, but not much, and most of the gear that they weren't wearing at the time was left behind. No bedrolls, little food, almost nothing beyond that. Thankfully, Kialor realized that one of the bags that Vishti had grabbed was his larger bag of healing supplies. They had at least a minor way to treat injuries, beyond what Sai'velk could do. She had the Risen One's power, but she didn't have the training that someone trained in the west would have.

Vishti urged her horse close to Kialor, gesturing toward where Evanira paced next to the party, still in the form of the great cat. "She's alright that way?"

Kialor shrugged, "I think she'll change back when she feels she needs to. Right now, she probably realizes that this gives us a little more of a chance. It frees up a horse from having to carry double. It means we can get away a little further before we need to take a rest. I just don't know where we can find a safe place for that, honestly."

Redel called back from where he rode ahead, "Kialor, I heard that. And I think that you're our best chance, anyhow. You've gotten safe-passage from the faedh before. That might be our only option. I don't think we should follow those who escaped the camp. If possible," he gestured toward the north-east, "I'd prefer a sanctuary in that direction. It's a risk, but I think I have to take that. We will be more likely to run into trouble, but I think that's still the best idea. And, perhaps, if we can find a faedh place, we can replace some of what we lost."

Kialor winced, the faedh. He'd already ended up owing them a service that hadn't fully come due, and now they were asking for another such thing. At least, theoretically, getting them into a sanctuary might be easier and less painful than asking for other help. "I'll try. We should go in that direction then, anyhow, and I'll see if I can find out more about that. Mother's better about such things, simply because of her background, but I might be able to get us some safety. Our horses at least are well fed and rested. They should carry us for quite a while."

Vishti rode a little closer, placing a hand on where his leg rested on the side of his saddle. "I have trust in you, Kialor. You knew to prepare, before the attack hit. You could tell more about me than I had realized. I had no idea that the Great Mother was seeking my mind."

Kialor nodded, then grimaced, “That’s one thing I can offer us that I couldn’t the Rhi’na’n. I can make us nearly invisible to the tah’nel. That’s what I’d done before, with Sihan’el, and I’ve improved that magic since I first attempted it. I should be able to make it carry a little further. It might make it harder to access resonant magic for now, but that might be a good idea. I know that, at the least, you, Vishti, Father, Sihan’el, Maskar, and Hela should be covered by it. Possibly Sai’velk as well. About the only ones of us that might be safe right now are myself and Evanira. I have no way of telling if Evanira needs such magic, honestly.”

Vishti nodded, “Try it on me first. It might give us a little more defense, since I’m the most open of us.”

He inclined his head and raised a hand, spinning off that magic quickly. Then directed his horse to move among the party, releasing such magic on each of the other riders, finally spelling Evanira where she paced beside the horses. He hesitated before trying to cast it on himself. Then decided it probably shouldn’t bother him. It wouldn’t interfere with his divine connection, and his mind might just be vulnerable. Though most of the scions of his family hadn’t been tested to have the tah’nel, that didn’t mean that he didn’t have at least a vaguely open one. He just might not know how to access it at this point.

His casting earned him a wry look from Maskar, merely a faint nod and the hint of a smirk. The dah'ral former thief seemed to find at least something amusing in the situation, but it wasn't obvious to Kialor yet what that might be. Only that something about the spell or about the need for it somehow caught Maskar in a lighter mood. Perhaps he was less affected by the situation. He wouldn't need to eat, only drink regularly while they came upon streams and pools. Otherwise, he just needed sunlight. That saved the team a little bit, but surely couldn't be all of what was on Maskar's mind. He'd been the one using the most energy, doubtless, with whatever resonant magic he'd used to make the earth itself rebel against the touch of the corpsefolk. That was magic that Kialor wasn't even sure he wanted to know where it came from, since it didn't seem to stem from any crystals.

Even as the party crested a hill to turn in the direction that Redel had indicated, Kialor could get a sense of what his mind had been seeking. He spurred his horse forward, moving even with Redel. "There is a place, and it seems currently unoccupied, which might be the best for us." He gestured toward a darkened area perhaps two candlemarks distant, in the lee of a rocky ridge. "We might be allowed in, though I'll have to lead when we get to the borders. And I'm going to have to have promises from the rest of you to be careful what you touch. In a sanctuary, even one that's currently abandoned, there are things that must be done, and other things that cannot be touched. I can tell that. But it requires people to listen to me."

Redel glanced at Kialor, almost giving a full belly laugh, "Son, do you honestly think there's anyone here who will disobey what you say, especially in a place like that? You've got more sense than most anyone else, and that's improved by your contact with the faedh themselves. If there's anyone who gives you any trouble, they'll be answering to me, if that makes any difference, but I think that even the two who are most likely to go their own way will listen to you in that case. They know the cost here. They also know that if there's a chance to pull us through this, it's probably going to require your mind. Now, maybe you should lead, and I'll keep to the rear, in case I need to get rid of anything following us. You've said that you made us invisible to the tah'nel, which means that anyone following us will have to find our tracks. We've got horses. It's not going to be impossible for them to track us, though I doubt they'll do it at any speed. I can use my voice, if necessary when facing anyone tracking us. Or my sword. Perhaps what Grandfather said is right, that soulswords are among the few weapons capable of taking down those of the Dead. I hadn't had a chance to try it, but we might have to, soon enough."

Kialor arched a brow. "I'd heard that you'd been able to cause some magic to leave a distinct impression on one of the Sisters once. Little left of her. If needed, perhaps you could draw magic from something one of us cast, if you need to do that again."

"That's clever, and very worthy of you. Charging my blade could likely have a stronger effect than I'd thought about. At least on one or two of the Dead. I couldn't do that against a horde of them, but if we can get them singly, it might be more effective than any other solution. You should trust yourself more, Kialor, if only because your insight works better than anyone else's here, except maybe Maskar's, and he's not telling me what his ideas are, not yet. I'm sure he has a few, but he's kept them to himself."

"I saw his amusement, when I was protecting everyone with my spell. I don't know why it was so funny, but it seemed to be. I wish I knew enough about our enemy to have some idea of what we might be facing here."

"Honestly, Kialor, I'd say almost anything might happen. We just have to adapt. If you have some means to determine the future, that would be another gift you could use. We just need to keep our minds working, and not let down our guard, not yet."

"Thank you, Father," Kialor managed, looking ahead at the path he'd decided upon. "I'm not used to people listening to me."

"That's because you liked to hide for so long. Now you can't. You are doing a very good job so far, and I think we can keep trusting you. But it does take getting used to. I know it. Now, get on ahead and lead us to this sanctuary." There was a clap on Kialor's back, and then a slap on the rump of his mount. Kialor shook his head, and took the lead position, for now.

Chapter 20

Hela waited at the edge of a darkened wood while Kialor went ahead, alone and on foot. She knew that the danger was great. She wasn't sure where other corpsefolk might be, but she was certain that there were more. Even if they'd put a score or more of them back to death, there were doubtless more of them ahead. She was on the edge of the group, looking out for potential danger, though she still had not reacquired the energy she'd spent both taking down a number of the Dead and destroying the wall of the cleft, making sure to limit the access the enemies would have to follow the group. There was a good chance that the enemy didn't know where the main entrance of the covert was, which would make it harder for the enemy to figure out where the Rhi'na'n had fled to.

Sihan'el moved in beside her, watching the area behind where they'd travelled with narrowed eyes. Hela hadn't realized, not until she saw how her husband had handled the influx of nearly indestructible enemies, that he was quite capable of using his mental gifts in some unique ways to try to slow down the Dead. He'd managed to not only throw fire at the enemy, but had altered the winds around his targets so that the fire had spread. It increased the range, which made it easier for Hela and Sai'velk to drop a few of the corpsefolk.

"I'm sure that Kialor will find out soon whether we're safe to go in," she offered to Sihan'el, where he seemed to be bouncing gusts of wind between his hands. "We'll get a chance to rest, for a little while, and make plans. I think we're going to need them, of course, because without the Rhi'na'n, we might not have a chance to take out the source of this danger."

His voice was very bitter as he responded. "You have no idea how much danger this is. I know that they've gone to the ruins of prior coverts. That's where they're getting the corpses for their magic. They were probably planning this before, though I didn't know it. I had no way to know it. The Rhi'na'n will have to flee, and still won't survive on their own. Unless we find some way to stop the Great Mother, the Dead will only increase, and it will be spread further. It might take time, but if the enemy can keep gaining mages, it will spread further, until it has all of us enslaved or killed."

"We'll find a way to overcome the enemy, Sihan'el. I don't know how you know that they're taking from your dead, but I believe you."

"I know, because I recognized some of the bodies. I'm dreading, honestly, the fact that we might face my brother's corpse, or perhaps that of others that we care about. If my son is dead, how will I be able to fight his corpse? I don't have the strength to set my fire against that, but I don't know if we'll have the choice. We will have to fight yet more of the corpsefolk. I don't have a chance to get away from this. I have to fight. It's the only thing that might give us a chance to get vengeance for our defiled kin. Right now, I'm not even sure I have a chance to look for a future, Hela. I just want to make the enemy pay, including my own mother, who I know is still among the kril'dga. I imagine Sai'velk's mother is serving the Great Mother still. I just want to make sure that this is stopped, even if it means my own death."

Hela almost froze as she remembered the dream that Sihan'el had had, before. She realized how disturbing it must be facing corpsefolk created from one's own kin or friends. It gave her chills to imagine what would happen if she'd seen a body she recognized among those. If she'd seen one of her brothers among them, or a niece or nephew. It produced a visceral reaction. It meant that for him, this fight was extremely personal. It meant that he wouldn't give up, not while there was life in him. He wanted to make sure that the Dead rested peacefully. She could understand that. She'd known ghosts for most of her life, thanks to a sister who could summon them. The idea that those ghosts could at least go for rebirth when they were ready was the only thing that made that tolerable. These corpses could not do that. They had no choice in their situation, and could not escape the horror that might be affecting their souls, especially if, as she'd heard, souls were still bound to bodies when such magics were used on the corpses. To be trapped within a body that did not obey your will, that would be horror indeed, especially if it was used to harm those that the soul had once loved.

"Sihan'el, I'm going to be at your side. Count on it. And not just because of our oaths. This thing that the enemy is doing is an abomination. We have to stop them. We just need to take the time to figure out how we are going to defeat the cause of this. It's about the only way to ensure that we succeed. And we have to succeed. If we don't, well, we'll be leaving behind those who cannot defend against this. We've got the only Singers here who can operate the method that was used to bring us here. And by the time that a larger force could be gathered, the Dead will be increased, and there will be no chance of defeating them. So we have to make sure that we do not lose. Which means that you need to try to survive. No matter what. As long as we're surviving, we have a chance to stop our enemy. And we have to make absolutely sure that she's stopped."

He bit his lip, chewed on it a moment, then glanced back over to her with only the slightest hint of a smile. "So, you understand exactly how dangerous this is. I can't imagine anything that would be more dangerous than that insane woman anymore. She had to have ordered this, ordered the summoning of the Dead. And she's likely to place the Dead where they will cause people to freeze, where the Sisters can't defend themselves. She wants to make us panic. And it's working. There's no way I can face what we'll be fighting without seeing Vashk's face, or Vedask's. I need to see the enemy dead, perhaps burn them myself. I can't stand the fear that this will come up again. If there was a way to do the mind burn against those who were doing this, I'd use it, no matter what it does to my soul."

"I know your bitterness, your fear and your anger, Sihan'el. I can only imagine what it would be like to face those you've known, as corpsefolk. I wish I could do something to erase this pain from you, but I can't. I can only fight at your side, just as everyone else here is going to do. I have little doubt that Kialor even is angry at what's going on. He understands what this does. He has strong feelings, even if he doesn't show them all the time. I am certain that Maskar and Evanira are just as angry. And I know that your father probably has the same feelings you do. He doubtless knows at least a few of the people who were raised. It will be just as bad for him, and possibly both of your sisters. We'll fight together. We have to. It's the only way we have a chance."

Almost as if she'd called for that change, Evanira moved up, on foot, but human again, or at least as human as Evanira was anymore. With the kee-ali-dahlri gifts she'd gained from the machine on the edge of the Steppe, she was no more human now than Hela's mother Denora was. The Dark Lands woman looked around, with just the hint of injuries from where she'd fought the Dead. She seemed just as capable as if she'd merely walked away from a normal practice. The only sense that she was disturbed was the way her fingers kept shifting between fingers and claws. And those claws were tipped by the same type of nails that she'd use in her tiger form.

"I sense that your nephew will be returning shortly," Evanira pronounced, wrinkling her nose. "While this place seems protected, there is something else here, something I'm not entirely sure about. We'll find out soon enough, however. We need to get someplace safe, soon. I think there are enemies coming, though they are not near, not yet. There was no way to hide our tracks, though perhaps my own will give the mages cause for distress."

Hela smirked, "Yes, I imagine many mages would be worried to see the tracks of a large hunting cat. They probably can still tell that we went here willingly, because the horses kept together. Whereas they might have run different directions if there hadn't been riders. So, yes, they'll know which direction we went in."

Evanira grimaced as she skimmed her vision over the land that they'd come from. Then, quietly, she spoke as she glanced at where Redel still sat on his horse, several feet away. "I think he intends to take us directly to danger. I do not know why, precisely, but he has plans. We will have to get him to tell us these plans, before we go much further. He may be our leader, but I think that he is keeping information from us, though I have never known him to do so before. I am less certain why he would think that we are not ready for such information, but he does keep things silent for now. I think that perhaps they weigh heavily on his soul. And that might be cause for alarm. Just as you have your fears, your angers and sorrows, so does he. And it might guide him wrongly as we progress."

Hela glanced over at Redel, shaking her head. "I'm sure he has good reasons for what he's doing, and, for now, I'm going to trust him. If only because he's proven himself sensible until now, even when I didn't expect him to be. You can watch him, but he has shown compassion and wisdom in ways I didn't have any reason to believe from him."

Evanira shrugged. "I will watch. But I still think he intends to lead us further into danger."

Sihan'el shook his head, "He might be leading us into danger. But, right now, that's where I want to go. Just to stop this." Hela couldn't help but agree silently.

Chapter 21

Vishti was grateful when Kialor seemed to merely appear out of the trees at the edge of this darkened wood. His face may have been grim, but he glanced at his horse and spoke a few words in the tongue she knew was from the Steppelanders, but didn't speak well, despite the transfer of languages. The horse moved beyond him, and he gestured to the others to dismount and follow. He said very little, and his face was streaked with sweat and dirt. Whatever it was that he'd faced within had allowed them to come, at least she hoped that was the case. She couldn't imagine anyone being able to use magic to control him to an extent that the horses would obey such controls. He had to still be in his right mind.

Vishti almost rushed to meet him, her face flushed with the need for something hopeful, after the terror she'd witnessed. She knew that the Dead were the Rhi'na'n, and possibly others who had been in this region, but she hadn't recognized faces, herself. She hadn't had enough of a chance to do so. But her ears had betrayed to her that her brother had recognized people, and the look on Father's face indicated some of the same. It was painful to think that the Dead were not left to rest, but there was nothing she could do about it, could she? If there was any chance at all of getting this to stop, it meant that they had to have a chance to recuperate, a chance to make plans that would leave the Mayisna vulnerable. She didn't expect those plans to require much thought from her. Yes, her gifts could be used, but they'd be used likely by another, perhaps her husband. If not, it would likely be her father or brother who did so, connecting with her so that the magic that was her birthright would be put to proper use. She couldn't do it, and only trusted that others could.

Kialor caught her, managed a wry smile and embraced her for only a few seconds, then he gestured to the wood beyond, not even taking her hand in his. That was painful, though she knew that he had to be under a great deal of stress right now. It made her almost stop where she stood. In fact, she might have, if it weren't for another coming to take her hand in theirs, urging her along with a faint nod. That the other was the sister she really didn't know didn't matter. It only meant that she needed the guidance once again.

The place beyond the edge of the trees was dim, not bright, and it smelled almost of mold and rot, a strange place for something dedicated to the nature spirits. When they got a little further within, near one of the few places where the sun shone through, Kialor shrugged, glanced at everyone, and cleared his throat.

"We can't stay here long, barely long enough to regain a bit of strength. By sunset, we'll need to be gone. I do have a bit of a hope, though. It's not one of their special pathways, but there is a way out that will almost certainly not attract attention, and it's going in the direction that Father wanted. We can take a bit of water, though not from the central pool, and a little bit, and only a little bit, of the fruits and berries near there," he gestured in the direction of a number of bushes and small trees hidden in near twilight. "We'll rest, maybe two candlemarks, and then I'd suggest we leave. This path will be a little bit faster, I think, than going over the open trail. But it's not going to be pleasant, I fear, not only with our exhaustion, but with a few other things."

"Other things?" Redel's voice had an edge to it even as he stripped down his horse, moving it toward one of the lesser springs. "You tell us we have a little luck, then hint ideas that may be too bleak."

Kialor shook his head, "They shouldn't be a threat, but they won't be easy to deal with. There's a good reason that the Dead and their controllers won't likely find us right away. It's a side effect of what created the corpsefolk in the first place. I learned more about that nature in a few minutes than I'd have wanted to learn in my entire lifetime. Creating corpsefolk fragments the souls of those who are raised. Only a small portion of that soul is with the body. The rest, well, it goes elsewhere, lost to pain and helplessness. Usually not too far, which indicates that the Dead may have been raised very near here. I think we might be able to calm those fragments. We have myself, Hela, and Sai'velk who can all contact to an extent with that nature. That's something that the mages who did this can't do. But what we are dealing with aren't whole souls, only bits and pieces. It will wear on our minds for as long as we're following the path. But, if we can at least calm them a bit, we'll have an advantage that the mages don't have. They don't dare bring the Dead close to that part of their souls. And they can't handle the madness that those souls would drive them to. So, we'll be unmolested for a while. How long, I don't know, just hopefully long enough to get us in the clear. I don't know what's beyond, and I can't judge where we're going, not yet."

Redel winced, "Partial souls? Did anyone tell you about what had happened to the Sa'eh? Or the ones they took to become that?"

Maskar shook his head, "I didn't tell him, Redel. If you didn't, he probably doesn't know. But, well, none of you were actually priests. It might make a difference. Brehl just has a means to alter magic to some degree, convince it to work for him. With three full priests, we might stand a chance that you didn't in Rigedh."

Vishti looked confused at Maskar and her father. "What are you talking about?"

"There was a place, not too long ago, a couple of years, really, where we encountered what happened when souls fragmented under serious torture. I didn't even think that that might be related to becoming corpsefolk. I'm not sure that Ael'yn, Yossa, or Brehl thought of it either. But if it does the same thing, well, we're not going to be comfortable, and I'm not sure how much we can shield our minds on that path. It might, in some ways, be more dangerous to us than facing the Dead themselves," Father commented, sighing. "I'm not sure I can handle that again."

Sihan'el tilted his head, "You think this thing with the souls of the Dead might be worse than the corpsefolk? I can hardly imagine that. I don't think I can face going up against people I knew in life again. I can't fight them, and I know we can't run far enough."

Vishti winced at this discussion. It certainly didn't sound good, though she could hear Sai'velk moving over in the direction of the fruit trees. "Sihan'el, isn't anything that gets us closer to our goal better than waiting to die?"

Kialor's words were rather cold, almost hollow with the pain he seemed to be experiencing. "That depends on what our goal is. Unless I know that, I'm almost worthless in finding the best and safest way for us all to get there."

Redel sighed, looked down. "You, none of you, will like this. I think our best bet is to make as straight a path as possible to the Fortress. We'll be tired, hungry, have little in the way of resources. But, unless something changes dramatically, it's the best chance we have to survive this, to bring safety to our peoples and our world."

Sihan'el was grim, but Evanira seemed angry from where she stood. "You would seek to have us battle when we have no strength, against enemies that outnumber us by many times? And you think that means that we will survive?"

Maskar reached out to touch Evanira's arm. She shrugged him off, causing him to almost recoil in fear and shock. Then came Father's voice again, filled with pain and hopelessness. "I think that it might be our only choice, Evanira. You're good, but we can't fight this. We have little in the way of supplies. That we have any I gather I have to thank my daughter for. We don't have the time to rest, because I imagine that the band of corpsefolk we fought aren't the only ones out there. Yes, Methil'dga is going to be dangerous. It's going to be extremely difficult to get into. But the kril'dga there are mortal. They can be killed by weapon or spell, and probably reasonably easily. We don't have that trust in defeating the corpsefolk. Even if the spell is only temporary, and it may be, to have raised so many so quickly, we can't count on being able to find those controlling the Dead. We can't be certain that they aren't hiding the mages who did this. We just have to outrun them. I'm hoping that they won't figure out where we're going. Especially if this path is hidden. We have a potential ally, too, who might be ready to help us get in, if we can find some way to contact her. I know Vishti probably won't want that, but if it's a chance, it's a chance, and we can't afford to ignore any of those. If we try going anywhere else, the Dead will just follow, expand, become more powerful. If we take down the source of the corruption, we have hope. It's a slim opportunity, but that's the best I can find at this point."

Kialor sighed, then nodded in Father's direction. "It is a chance. Even without an inside ally, I might be able to get you in. It just might take me doing something unexpected during our short rest here. I think, if I'm right, that I can use either Sai'velk's memory, or Vishti's, which she doubtless doesn't think she has, to determine the best ways in. I can't get lost. I can find those entrances again. We just have to hope that they're still mostly secret. It could give us a chance we don't otherwise have."

Vishti looked at her husband in confusion. "I didn't know those passages. I was told that I was lost to all knowledge at that time."

"They're there. I saw hints before. I can look for those hints now. But we need to rest. Let's get the horses to graze, and what grain we have. Then we'll sit down, and I'll see what I can do. And everyone except Maskar needs a share of food. We can't guess when our next meal will be, so we need to make sure to make the best of what's here now." It was said with a clear note of sadness, but Vishti had reason to hope that her husband had options up his sleeve yet. He had to.

Chapter 22

Sihan'el guided his horse slowly through a path where the sun seemed almost too dim, though Maskar was not yet complaining about the lack of sunlight that he was dealing with. It might get worse if they had to press on after dark. There were smells of rot and moss here, decay of various types. There was a near constant murmur that he thought, initially, was the wind. As they progressed, however, he realized that they were not. They were snatches of conversation, just bits and pieces, a statement here, a cry there, whispers just on the edge of what he could hear. No one else seemed to look up at them, though Father, from where he rode near the front of the party, seemed distressed. He had prior experience in this, from what Sihan'el gathered. None of the others did, though they seemed to be functioning reasonably well. Sihan'el wondered, just a bit, if he was the only one who heard these voices, but guessed that that wasn't the case. It only meant that the others were better at drowning them out with their thoughts.

It was getting late, and they'd been on the road again for at least two more candlemarks. Soon they'd have to find a place to camp, because it would be too dark to keep the horses moving, and, honestly, with as far and as fast as they'd gone, no one would be capable of much else for a while. Father seemed to be thinking that, since he'd moved over to consult with Kialor. Kialor pulled something out, and seemed to look into it, while his horse kept plodding along, then shook his head. The words he said were audible to everyone.

"There are corpsefolk almost lining this valley, on both sides. It's almost like they're waiting for us. In fact, I suspect they are. I can't tell why, but that seems to be what's in the pattern right now. As if our enemies know exactly where we are. That doesn't make any sense to me. And it won't be too long before we're out of range of the Dead who guard us now."

Redel's voice showed the strain that Sihan'el felt. "You're sure that they know we're here? There's no way that they should be able to do that, not if your spell from earlier is still functioning. I guess they might have mages who can scry, but I'm guessing that's not likely, not without some good reason to know who we are, and what we're doing. You said before that the Mayisna might have been looking through our minds, but I'm not sure that's the case. I know at least that my mind is shielded by the Goddess, and I think that's the same for you, Hela, and Sai'velk. Vishti might still be a weak link there, but I'm not sure. And Hela should have noticed if Sihan'el had had his mind invaded. Just like you should have known faster with Vishti."

Sihan'el winced at the thought that he might have indirectly led the enemy to their encampment. He thought that yes, Hela should have known. She had her mouth on his often enough that any traces of contact should have been visible to her. And with her god-guided senses, she should be more than aware of such traces.

Kialor's voice, however, from what Sihan'el could hear, sounded confused. "That's it. I'm not sure that the Mayisna was using Vishti at all. My contact with her awareness seemed more like the fact that Vishti and the Great Mother existed in the same place, in a way. But neither was touching the other, until I just happened to brush against her awareness, probably one of my instincts that you are relying on. My instinct is that we're missing something. And yes, my spell should protect anyone from being sensed through the tah'nel."

Redel frowned, "Check everyone, now. I get a feeling that this is something we need to know. If necessary, have Hela try sensing for problems in your own mind. She's likely gotten the experience for it."

Kialor nodded, calling a halt where they were, and moving through the group, something held in his hand as he looked at everyone with some form of magic running. Then his eyes narrowed, and he pointed to Evanira, where she sat behind Maskar on his horse. "Get down, now, Evanira. We need to check something." His voice was hard, and almost instantly Father was on the ground, reaching out for the ebon skinned warrior woman. It was a tense moment before Evanira dropped from the horse, grimacing at the others.

Maskar looked down at them, Redel, Kialor, and Evanira, and raised a hand to stop things. "What's wrong? Why do you need Evanira?"

Kialor reached out, taking Evanira's wrist, then looked at Maskar. "You've got one of the strongest minds in here. I need you to search hers. If necessary, Father and I will hold her. I think, perhaps, because my spell was on the cat, it might have had a different effect."

Evanira seemed to grimace, but did not pull away from Kialor, possibly because Redel was physically stronger, and possibly because Kialor had other magics, maybe even magics that could chain her. Maskar got down, moved around to look at Evanira, then shook his head, "I have to do this, luv. I don't know how you might be vulnerable, but they think you are." Then, slowly, deliberately, he kissed her.

Sihan'el could watch the expression on his face from where he still sat on his horse. It was a mixture of distaste, then shock, then some form of forceful push, though not physically. As he pulled back, Kialor was throwing a spell out, seemingly having guessed it. The words that the priest asked, however, as he finished were almost scarier. "How long?"

Maskar shook his head, "Perhaps since before the attack on the keep. It's hard to tell. I know she's had some dreams, off and on. I thought that they came from the attack, but this seems older, perhaps from shortly after we were studying her gifts."

Evanira pulled, and this time, Kialor let her go. Her face was livid. "So, what are you going to do, since you obviously think I'm a traitor?"

Redel shook his head, "You're not a traitor, at least not willingly. But I'd like to know how she got to you. It might give us a means to undo some of this harm, at least with you. She took knowledge from you, almost certainly including the identity of the ally I was hoping would still be safe. I doubt she is, now. Not unless she's cleverer than I thought. She might be. I think, though, that that's probably not all the Great Mother did to you, Evanira. Tell us about the dreams. We'll stay here until we know what best to do."

Sihan'el could sense Hela moving her horse over to right beside him. She seemed nervous, though Sihan'el couldn't see why, particularly. The priestess at least had not been implicated in anything. She merely was watching the scene play out.

Evanira spat out her answer, looking at Maskar. "You had her father taken, probably killed. I saw that, in the memories she showed. You act as if she's a monster, but I'm beginning to wonder if all of you might be, now. She was a little girl who wouldn't have done any of this if she'd been left in the care of her only family."

Maskar blinked, then grimaced. "Her father vanished, but we didn't have anything to do with that. Virea did have her taken from his care, for her own reasons. But he was allowed to visit, and did, regularly. When he disappeared, the first thing Virea did was guard her more securely, then send someone to investigate his projects from before, the reasons why she'd taken Mi'la. They'd been closed since the day Mi'la had been taken. There had been no work there at all. She investigated the other dah'ral, expecting a power play. No one knew what happened to him. When we searched his quarters, only one thing remained that couldn't be understood, a crystal with two images, images that drove the first person to try to link with it absolutely insane. I saw them, though it was painful to me, in that other life. I saw that there was an image that shifted between a woman and an infant. When the image was that of an infant, there was a hint of two other people, a man and a woman, but no more than a hint, no image itself. The other thing in there was probably what drove our assistant insane.

"What was in there can't even begin to be described in words. It's like power, raw and pulsing, but also colors, light, sound, all mixed with the intent of causing madness. It didn't answer where he'd gone, or how he'd done so. We don't know what happened to her father, but I assure you, it wasn't because of either myself or Virea, well, who we were in those lives. We only know that he vanished, and, after that, Virea did her best to protect the child. It didn't work."

Almost unexpectedly, Vishti spoke, from a position a little behind Maskar's horse. Her words didn't make much sense, but they didn't seem insane, either. "She called him. Not as she was then, but elsewhere. It was a place where time and space don't matter, where everything is, all at once. She knows it, remembers it. I don't know how I understand it, but I do. It was something impossible."

Maskar looked at Vishti, as did Kialor. Then they both shook their heads. Maskar was the first to speak. "That sounds like when she was imprisoned. I'm not sure how that could do anything about what had happened when she was young, about five years old. I can't say you're wrong, but I don't understand it."

Kialor's voice was harder, "You're not meant to. I think it's only for her to understand. Remember what Uncle Telin did, back in Sharlan. I think she knows something, but can't expand on it. Which might be for the best, for now."

Maskar reached out, offering a hand to Evanira. "Just as your mother didn't want to leave you, but was taken by the Sa'eh, I think this was much the same. He was taken, but not because of us, even as we were, which weren't the best of people, then. Now, since Kialor has done something about your mind, to protect you, can we get a move on? I think we need to find someplace safe, even if it means we have to do something unexpected."

She took his hand, then Kialor nodded, and glanced at Sai'velk, of all people, "Perhaps we should use your method. It might just give us an advantage." He didn't explain, but Sihan'el realized that perhaps Kialor was capable of keeping secrets. Another path was one that had been kept very well.

Chapter 23

Kialor wasn't entirely sure this would work when he suggested it, but it was about the only solution he could see for getting them out of their predicament. He'd whispered to Sai'velk, when he'd taken the knowledge from her in the kiss that he'd needed for navigation, that he needed this to stay silent for now. He was fairly certain that she wasn't the source of the luck that had led the Great Mother to find their encampment, but he couldn't be certain that no one else among them was. Yes, there had been a chance that it might have been one of the girls that they'd rescued, but he had the instinct that it wasn't. An instinct that might save their lives now.

It would be tricky, from where they were, to do this, but he had reason to believe it might work, the means to get them to where they could bypass the corpsefolk that surrounded the section of forest they were in. It would require misdirection, and some pretty powerful misdirection at that. They had to give the enemy reason to believe that they were someplace that they were not. Right now, Kialor had to trust that Maskar would be able to sense, now that he knew the danger of Evanira's mind, if the Great Mother was still tracking them through it. For the rest, well, that was where he just hoped he could handle things properly.

A part of that required them to double back, toward the faedh shelter. Amazingly, that shelter was not far from a series of caves that had hidden Sai'velk as she'd fled from Methil'dga. If they could give an impression that they were pressing on, the enemy might not think of looking back for them. It might be difficult to keep the horses. In fact, it might be wisest to send them back to the faedh sanctuary, as they would be safest there, but it would be a place that likely did not include any of the Dead. And those passages were twisted and mysterious, crossing each other at many points, which would confuse anyone who was not very familiar with them, or who didn't have the same gift that all of Lady Night's called servants had, the ability to determine direction and distance to anyplace they were familiar with. Kialor was taking a risk. He was fairly certain that he could take those locations from Sai'velk's and Vishti's minds, and still be able to use them for this gift. If it worked, it would take them completely out of where the enemy might expect, giving them another option to get to the Fortress.

To pull this off, he needed Hela's gifts. She might not be especially trained in deception, but deception was something that her Lord controlled to some degree. In this, he shared it with Kialor's own Lady, who used deception to further her own ends, fixing the Tapestry of Fate, a tapestry that was now whole, since their Music had been successful. Hela's magic could be directed, Kialor was fairly sure, to appear in a different location than she was at. If she could do that, it would guide the enemy to the opposite direction, leaving them a gap to get through to the caves. And those were caves he suspected were still quite secret. At least he hoped so. He was risking all of their lives to pull this off.

Moving over to Hela, he gestured down the path they'd intended to take, "I need you to do something rather challenging, especially for you. I need you to make it seem like we're where we aren't. I can hide us, reasonably well, but I need it to seem that we're still heading in the same direction, preferably for a while. Give them a reason to go in that direction. Then we'll use what strength we have to go back toward the sanctuary. There's another way, not far from there, and if we can get rid of our followers, we can sneak through to that fairly well. But, the last leg of the trip we need to leave our horses, send them back to the sanctuary. They'll be safe there. We'll be going underground, so they won't do nearly as well there. If we survive, I'll see what we can do to retrieve them. But we're also more likely to be able to hide on foot, if we have to."

Hela pursed her lips, but did not argue immediately. She took a moment to center herself, fingering the medallion that was carved with the image of a serpent coiled around a scimitar. After a moment, Kialor could feel something change, some image of himself and the others going down the way they'd originally intended. It might have been weak, but he couldn't ask for anything more. It was only a mental image, not a physical illusion, but it might be enough, since it would attract the mages in that direction, and the Dead would merely follow commands. He hoped it would give them enough time to travel back to the caves.

Then, looking over his shoulder, "We have to hurry. That won't buy us too much time. Now, everyone, back the way we came. We've got a chance, but not a good one. I'm just hoping that the caves that I'm thinking of might have escaped detection. Or at least serious exploration."

He glanced over to where Sai'velk was sitting in front of her brother, on his horse. He hoped this wouldn't be too hard on her, since she wasn't familiar with riding very well, and would have to depend on someone else. But they had to hurry. And he urged his beast to run, despite the darkness of the forest, back toward the sanctuary. If he did this right, they'd have a chance to rest, safely. They might end up losing the saddles, good ones that Grandfather Caldor had made, but that was better than letting the horses run with them. That could harm the horses, especially if there were no faedh in the area who might tend them.

The sense of danger seemed to fade, as the horses hurried through the darkening forest. Kialor was tired, exhausted, really, but knew that they had to keep moving. They couldn't even stop once they'd gotten into the caves. Once the enemies discovered the ruse, they'd be looking for other paths that the party could have taken. Those caves might be reasonably well hidden, but they weren't impossible to find. And even with the twisty passages, there likely were enough of the Dead to let them just overwhelm the caverns searching for the party. It also meant that he'd have to use magic on the last leg of the journey to the caves, to conceal any sign that that's where they were going. He couldn't trust that magic to anyone else, largely because he was the only one here with significant experience with the faedh. His use of their methods would make it almost impossible to detect where they'd come out, and where they were headed.

There, that seemed about the right place, his mental senses told him. He pulled to a stop, signing for people to dismount and remove the saddles from their mounts. None of the horses had bits to their bridles, merely halters that should not hinder them, though the reins would have to be removed, so that none of the horses could get itself caught on the bushes or plants nearby. It was a risk that he didn't want to take. These animals had served them well. At the very least, they should be given a chance to survive, perhaps thrive, even if none of the people survived this battle. And that was a very good chance still.

Hela shook her head, "We'll need at least one. Mine will do. I can walk him, but we may need to draw someone off as we're heading to the caves. I can remove the saddle, but I'll still have him handy if we need speed for someone. He knows what he's doing, and can make it back to the sanctuary, if you tell him what to do. I just am not abandoning him here."

"It would be for the best, Hela. We don't know how much time we have."

"Then we shouldn't waste time arguing. I'm not leaving him. You should know not to press me on this, not for any reason."

Kialor sighed, glanced at both Sihan'el and Redel, and saw that both shrugged. He just hoped that the horse wasn't so visible when they reached open ground. He pulled the bags off of the saddle he was riding, throwing them over his shoulders, and watched as everyone did the same. Then they hid the saddles under some bushes, concealing them as best as they could, and Kialor took the lead again, murmuring his magic to control the visibility of the group, and to wipe away any tracks that they might leave. It wasn't going to be easy, because they still had a good stretch to go, but it was twilight. All of them had the ability to see well in the starlight, and shouldn't need light. Hela's horse would have to trust her, because they wouldn't be creating any extra light for him to see by. Hopefully, they could pass unseen, but he really wasn't counting on it.

There was a sense of interest, as if the faedh were not far, even if they were not in their sanctuary. Perhaps it was because of Hrif, who flew on ahead, despite the difficulty for her to see where she was flying, and the possibility of becoming prey of a night flying creature, such as an owl. But Hrif also had faedh magic about her. Perhaps she could hide herself from normal sight. Perhaps she could merely direct the owls away. The faedh might protect the little bird. Kialor only hoped that they would protect his family as well. They desperately needed to be able to do this.

The path was clear for a while, but there was still a faint odor of decay, a sense of distress. It grew closer as they approached the area where the caves were hidden. Hela's stallion became more nervous, but Kialor couldn't tell why, not yet. It wasn't the Dead, but something else. Then, just as he could make out the area where the caves were hidden, he got a better sense for it. There were vines that weren't there when Sai'velk had left the place, years ago. Those vines were the source of the smell, and they seemed to have a darkness around them. But there was no other choice now but move toward them.

Chapter 24

Hela could tell that something was making Kialor nervous before she saw it. And, if she hadn't known to watch for his reaction, she wouldn't have known that much. There was a mass of vines covering what likely was that cave. Examining it with her God-given gifts, she realized that it pulsed with both life and death. It made her wary, though she kept following Kialor, one hand on the back of her stallion. She really didn't want to leave him, even if he could get back to the faedh sanctuary. He'd been nearly the only companion she could count on for many years, since there were few that trusted anyone who served the Serpent Lord. The stallion was comfortable, familiar, in a way that Sihan'el really wasn't yet.

Kialor moved more cautiously as he neared the small hidden area where the cave was located. He stood well back from the vines, then shifted languages to something that Hela was only vaguely familiar with. She knew that some of her family were quite familiar with the faedh, though she herself was not. That he was speaking in it indicated that there was something both aware and dangerous about this vine. Then she heard the answer, in oddly accented Trade, which meant that Sai'velk might have been left in the dark about the nature of this trial.

"Blood and pain are required to pass. That will be true of those following, even as it will be for you. There are no other options open to you. A sacrifice must be made." Simple, straightforward, and utterly impossible. Was the thing asking for one of her companions, or herself, to die, just to open the passage beyond?

Kialor frowned, glancing through the group before turning his attention back to the wall of vines. "We will not sacrifice one of our own, as we will all be needed. Beyond my own family, there are only two with us that are perhaps not as needed, the gift I was given when I learned the arts of the faedh, and the horse that Hela holds."

"Life's blood, and pain are all that is needed. It need not be of your own kind. But all other creatures have been chased from here, by the Dead that will catch you if you do not move quickly."

Redel spoke up, looking at Kialor, "While Hrif won't be as useful in the tunnels, at least not without light, the horse will be even more of a detriment. We have no choice, as the faedh says. We have to get past here, and quickly. Doubtless they've figured out that we aren't where we were expected to go by now."

Hela turned on her cousin, eyes blazing, "You're suggesting that I turn over my horse? What benefit is that thrush anyhow?"

"That thrush," the knight replied, "can guide us, scout for us, and remain mostly unseen. Given enough light to work by, it will serve us better than your horse will. Perhaps you were right, bringing him with us. Right now, we need him, to offer the faedh. It offers us a chance that we desperately need. I know how that hurts you, especially with how you've cared for him, but this isn't something that we can debate, and you know it, Cousin. Ask your husband, if you must. He's lost a brother, maybe a son, to this. He knows what it feels like. I imagine he'd suggest the beast's death, just to give us a chance to stop other deaths, including your own. If he dies now, we have a chance at survival. If he doesn't, we'll likely all die, including him. Now, do you understand the predicament we're in?"

Hela could see Sihan'el wince, then nod, "He's right. Right now, this is what we need. I know it will hurt, but it's what we need to do. If the faedh is right, we have no other choices that will work. Perhaps, with this sacrifice, we'll be able to get into the Fortress and you'll have your chance at revenge. I know that's what you'll want. It's what I want too, and possibly my father as well. We need to do this."

Hela buried her face in the stallion's mane, not wanting to face this. But, with a vague sense of understanding flickering from her contact with her god, she pulled her face away, turning to look at the vine thing. "If this happens, I'll do it. You'll have his blood, and my pain. But I won't let him suffer. I can't do that. If you have any idea of what I am in nature, you'll know that. I can't make a horse suffer."

There was a hint of amusement, though how she could read that she wasn't sure. "That is agreeable. Bring him to me, and use your blade. I can draw from the pain in your spirit, and that will open these passages. You will be permitted onward. If you go swiftly, it will be more difficult for your enemies to find you. They will have to make the same sacrifices, and the Dead can grant neither pain nor blood. They do not know where these caves go, and that will allow you a degree of safety. But you must do so quickly, for they are only a few miles away."

Hela bit her lip, then rubbed at the stallion's nose. Then, gently, she coaxed him over to the vines, speaking softly, asking him to forgive her. "Come on, old boy. I won't let this hurt. I know you trusted me, and I'm doing the worst thing possible, killing you myself. But it's for the best. You would die otherwise, and I understand that, even if I can't face it myself."

She drew her knife, since it would be cleaner than her claws, and lifted the beast's head with one hand. It seemed too calm, like it understood that she had no choice. Then, filled with anguish that threatened to crush her, she slid the knife into the skin, piercing the veins that brought blood to the horse's brain.

It was as if her hands were moving through molasses, because they had taken on a lethargy that she couldn't control. She could feel the sticky fluid wash over her hands and knife, then pool at her feet. Thankfully, the stallion didn't rear, it didn't fight her. It allowed her to kill it, with the kind of trust that she'd built up in it over the past decade. The pain in her heart was enormous, almost debilitating. She found herself falling, sinking to her knees next to the pool, only to be held by someone who did nothing more than wrap his arms around her and whisper in her ear. It took her a long moment to realize that that was her husband, already trying to do more for her than she had expected when they'd made their agreement toward marriage. This was not the first time he had come to her, tried to make things better. She'd never asked for that, but found that she needed it. And he seemed to know that, even if he didn't know anything more about the situation.

The faedh seemed to brush a vine tendril against her, and she could feel a bit of the pain recede, allowing space for the emotion that would be necessary to continue. That emotion was anger, hatred, toward those who had allowed this situation to occur. The Mayisna, her highest placed claws, those were the enemy. And she would see this battle ended, blood spilled to pay for the blood she'd had to spill today, blood of someone who had trusted her utterly and she'd had to betray, just so that everyone else could survive. It was all that she could face at the moment. And the anger only grew, causing her to stand up, looking straight at the vines, her face awash with blood and tears.

"The sacrifice is accepted, and the way will be opened to you. Remember, child, that there are good reasons for the prices we ask. In this, by demanding a price of you, we make it harder for your enemy to find you. The other understands this, knows what the value is of what is being asked." The faedh moved the tendrils, opening a way into the cavern beyond. It was only as it did so that Hela could see that the vines were tipped with sharp, perhaps poisoned, thorns.

Sihan'el did not leave her, though he let her pull herself from his arms. He offered a gourd of water to wash her hands with. She shook her head. "I will bear this stain, for now, as a testament of what I've had to do, the sacrifices I've had to make for this to work."

She could hear Kialor clear his throat, but it was Redel who answered that. "All of us have had to make sacrifices, Hela. Yours just had to be of blood. We need to get moving, to make use of the time this has granted us. Come on. We shouldn't stand here much longer. You did it well, made sure that the suffering was yours, not the horse's. That's the way it should be, and we both know it. You really have earned your Lord's favor tonight, I think, because doubtless he knows what this cost, and will find a way to suitably reward you later."

Sai'velk moved past her, seeming to draw up a glow to light the passage ahead. That she was herself the light seemed to matter little. Hela wondered absently how long it would be that the priestess could hold the phoenix fire, especially after the dangers they'd already faced. Perhaps it didn't matter. Redel had crystals, as did Maskar, taking basically all of the selection that had been in the Rhi'na'n camp, after finding that there was no Singer who could use them among the survivors of earlier raids. They would have light. And they had to move.

Hela passed under the vine curtain, trying to make a promise with each step she took that she would have revenge for the death of her beloved horse. That those promises didn't have words, she didn't care, only focused on that as she pushed herself further ahead.

Chapter 25

Vishti knew what Hela was going through, but wasn't sure what she could do to help. Kialor had led them deep into the bowels of these caves, and had taken them to an odd place that seemed amazingly well obscured from the rest of the tunnels. It was a good thing, too, because none of them, including Vishti herself, who was still very accustomed to long walks, was likely going to be able to continue without a rest. Even with the enemy behind them, they couldn't keep moving, especially if they had to fight again.

Kialor spent a few moments at each side of the passage, working on an illusion that would conceal them from nearly anything. How he retained enough power to do that, she didn't know, but she was grateful. And even more grateful that this section of cavern was big enough that everyone could lay down. Vishti dropped off the packs she had, and almost immediately wrapped herself up in her cloak. It wasn't as good as lying in a bedroll, especially with the idea of being held by her husband, but it would be adequate for now. While they had food, she felt that it was best waiting until they'd rested before trying to eat any, and before they drank anything more than a mouthful of water to clear the throat.

She was surprised to find that no one moved away, and no one was going to stand watch. They probably needed a guard, but for whatever reason, no one was taking on that responsibility. Then her father's words made sense of that. "Your thrush will notify you if anything gets close?" He was speaking to Kialor.

"If it gets that close. I have other means that will alert me earlier than that, most likely. As you have your sword. Between those three things, we should be able to handle an emergency should it happen. Right now, we have more of a chance if we all rest now, and so don't have to delay as someone else is taking a rest. We should all stay close together, too, both for warmth, since we have no blankets, and for emotional comfort. I imagine that all of us need to remember that we're not alone. It's not been a good day for anyone, and nightmares are likely. If we stay together, well, we'll likely grant enough comfort that we'll rest reasonably well, in spite of the troubles. Exhaustion should help, too."

That was something that Vishti understood. Even though there were three couples, and her father and sister, it would make a lot of sense for everyone to curl up together. Father would have to be on one end, because of his sword, but it would grant a lot more of a feeling of being loved than anyone sleeping completely alone. And since they'd only be able to curl up in their cloaks, they wouldn't be undressing really at all. It just wasn't safe to.

Almost surprisingly, Vishti found that Sihan'el was placing Hela next to her, with him on the other side. Knowing that Kialor would agree, Vishti snuggled up against Hela, offering her a completely non-judgmental acceptance that might do the priestess good. If she knew that she was loved, perhaps she could remove herself from the darkness that lay in her soul, especially after having to kill something she'd loved so deeply. That in and of itself made certain things clear in Vishti's head. Sihan'el had been right to block Vishti when she'd seen her mother. Knowing what she did now, Vishti held no hatred for the one she'd thought so long had betrayed her. What had happened hadn't been an intentional wrong, but choosing the lesser of two wrongs. And, despite the pain she'd held so long, Vishti realized that she now wanted her mother to survive the coming battle, if only so that Vishti could let her know that she was forgiven. It was a gift that would be not only to Sah'lev'da'kril, but to Vishti herself.

Kialor seemed to understand at least a bit of what Vishti was doing, and placed one arm under her head, with the other draped over her body. It felt both solid and familiar, something that she hoped to be able to feel for perhaps centuries to come. But that depended on whether they could survive this. There was a chance, a very good chance, that one or more of the group would fall in trying to defeat the Mayisna. It wasn't going to be easy to fight the Great Mother, but it was necessary, for the world as a whole. They needed to make sure that her power was quenched. But, Vishti realized, perhaps not her life.

Hela seemed to shudder where she was lying, not yet quite ready to sleep. Vishti could vaguely hear Sihan'el murmur to her, trying to soothe the pain that would not go away. Vishti realized that almost no one, including Hela herself, likely knew what to expect of Sihan'el. Vishti knew, though. She'd felt her brother do something like this decades ago, when she'd been retrieved from the dungeons under Methil'dga. He'd been extremely gentle, vulnerable. He'd shown Vishti his heart, in ways that perhaps he'd shown it to no one else, until now. He likely hadn't had a chance to show it to Vashk before, if only because the boy was elsewhere much of the time. She was fairly certain that Sihan'el hadn't really cared for the woman who'd borne his son. For the two of them, it had likely only been business. What Sihan'el felt for Hela, though, was different.

Gently, the tremors beside her subsided, and Vishti drifted off into sleep, a sleep that contained an awareness outside of time. She wasn't sure where she'd gotten this. Some of it, she'd had for longer than she'd known Kialor. Some, though, was newer, likely the product of the information that she'd been given by the man she'd been told was Uncle Telin. She only knew that she understood reality in a way that none of the others seemed to understand, even Kialor, who was usually so good at reading her. He'd made mistakes in that, too, but never big ones, never ones that cost. Almost always, when he misjudged her, it was that he expected the pain to overwhelm her. When it didn't, there was less to worry about.

Tonight's dream made an eerie sort of sense to her, from the story she was told part of by Maskar and Evanira earlier, and what Vishti herself had somehow known. She still didn't know how she knew that. Kialor had asked her, briefly, while they were travelling. She could only tell him that she knew it to be true, just had no idea how she knew it. He didn't seem to take that amiss, perhaps because he himself had to trust so much to his instincts, his ability to simply know things without realizing what had guided him to that knowledge. That made it easier to admit to him that she wasn't sure of the origin of the knowledge, only was certain that it was in fact true.

She could see someone, a man, his face seeming haggard and drawn, fighting against a mental compulsion that she could only vaguely sense. She could see him pacing a stone room, muttering to himself. She could see that when he slept, it was with the fitful dreams that gave little rest. Then, she saw that he determined to answer whatever it was that was calling him. He opened himself to something, something that she couldn't put into words, only accept, something that seemed to rip him from reality. It brought him to a place beyond knowledge, a place where they said that the Mayisna herself had been imprisoned for millennia. But, his stay there was different. She couldn't say why, but that it wasn't as much a case of him staying there, but stepping from one point of our world to another. He simply wasn't continued in that strange place, but, by someone who knew how to do it, he could, perhaps, be called to our world again, emerging as if he'd just travelled down a hallway.

She was right in considering that place beyond the world to be different in ways that she described as being beyond time and space. But there was more to it than that. Anything could be brought to any point in its existence, with little more than a thought, if you knew what you were doing. She wasn't sure, yet, that she knew that, but she realized that her mind was much more capable of perceiving this nature than anyone else. She had an insight into this reality that was beyond even that of one who had been there physically and returned. She understood, in ways that could not be explained, exactly what this reality was capable of. She only needed to decide how to use that, productively. That would be the trick. If she could do so correctly, she might make the need for battle less, perhaps remove it completely. But she also knew that if she did it wrong, she could erase herself and her family from existence in entirety. Perhaps worse damage than that.

In her mind, she could hear distant weeping. It wasn't Hela, who was sleeping more or less peacefully next to her. No, she was fairly certain that she was hearing the Great Mother weep, and that those sobs were, in a way, those of a frightened child, someone who had never had the chance to really get to know comfort, get to know love. She'd had the only one she loved reft from her, even if it was by her own more adult mind. The Mayisna was sad, lost, needing nothing so much as nurturing aid. If what Telin had said was true, perhaps they could have done more, if they hadn't been suddenly made busy by the arrival of a pair of twins. Perhaps, if someone had taken the time then, there might have been healing. But she knew that healing was possible, eminently possible. It just took understanding what caused the pain, the loss, and the fear. With those thoughts, Vishti found herself calming, relaxing, sensing that perhaps things weren't as bad as they seemed.

Chapter 26

Sihan'el knew that Hela was still aching, though she said nothing during what counted as breakfast. She had been hard to console, in part because he could not console her physically, something which might have given her the opportunity to heal. That was really impossible in this situation, even if he'd been inclined to try, or if she'd been inclined to accept it. He knew that a part of her still considered him complicit in her stallion's death. He'd spoken up to convince her, even though he knew that it would be one of the hardest things she'd likely ever do. There just had been no other choice, and hopefully she would come to understand it, as time went by. He just didn't count on it happening anytime soon.

Kialor let Redel light the area with enough light, through resonant magic, to see by, and they progressed through the tunnels. Sihan'el had considered that they might be more than a day away from the Fortress, but the priest shook his head, saying that he was fairly certain that there was a shorter way, one that avoided the obstacles that existed on the surface. They would still be walking, which slowed things, but Kialor had gotten a sense for where they were, and pointed out that they were a lot closer to the outer walls of that place, through his ability to sense direction and distance, than Sihan'el had realized. They were under a part of the mountainside that divided the Rhi'na'n camp from the Fortress already.

The passage was dusty, largely unused, but there was no sign of the Dead in it. Perhaps, indeed, the direction that Kialor had taken them in, almost over the objections of Sai'velk, who seemed to think another path might be better, was enough to keep them from attracting attention from their enemies. It led him to wonder what else his sister's husband was capable of, since determining information seemed to be a skill that most warriors neglected. But, from what Sihan'el gathered, that was largely what the faith of Lady Night did, gather information to make the best decisions possible when going up against threats or difficulties.

There was a sound of water ahead, which was something Sihan'el had not been counting on. The water was a little way distant, but not too far, though the caves distorted it. That would be a blessing indeed, since they had little enough in the way of food or water, and perhaps, though Sihan'el wasn't too familiar with it, there would be things within the caves that they could eat, somehow replenish their supplies a bit. Not that they were guaranteed a chance to use those supplies, especially if the Fortress was within a day's travel on foot.

Sihan'el followed obediently as they were led toward the water, finding, much to his surprise, that it was more than just a cavern here, but something else entirely. Some of this had been cut, hewn, though a very long time ago. It looked like it was older than the deepest chambers in Methil'dga, at least the ones he'd been to. There were carvings among the stones, and the river that cut through it was clean and pure, almost as if it had been spelled that way. Sihan'el glanced at Kialor questioning, but the other did little more than shrug.

"You can't have found this on accident," Sihan'el almost accused him. "And Sai'velk seems like she's never seen this place."

"She hasn't. She entered these caves in another direction. But this is what I was hoping to find. It just made too much sense. And, while we were eating, I did a little scrying. I realized that there was a set of actual passages here, and that they probably have a secret entrance into areas that the Mayisna herself may not know. Methil'dga predates her, in some ways, though much of it was rebuilt since that. Things that Uncle Telin said a long time ago make sense now. She was banished to the other place from a place deep in Methil'dga, which meant that it had to already be in existence. That being said, things Maskar has said about the underground workings of ancient Singers made it make a lot of sense that there are other ways in. Sai'velk confirmed it, though she might not have realized it. The way she entered wasn't quite the same as what we're looking for. It was secret, but not in the same way. I'm still going by instinct, but I think that we can get into the fortress from a direction they're not expecting. And, well, I think that there are other things moving up there. I haven't been told what, yet, but I imagine we'll find out soon enough."

Father spoke up, "That's thinking, and thinking that I hadn't been doing. I know of the fact that there were areas of the fortress supposedly sealed up, long ago, but I didn't realize that they might be fairly easy to unseal, if we do this right. And those are going to be just where the enemy doesn't expect us to come from. This will include rooms below the crystal chamber, and indeed, there might be a passage directly to that. A surprise attack, and one that will demoralize them, considering where it's coming from."

Kialor led the way along the side of the river, toward an area that seemed to be cut into a canal of sorts. He seemed to be looking for something in particular, though, when it happened, it was Maskar who found it, a broad grin forming over his unearthly pale face. "A boat, Kialor? Speeding the way, since we can handle it easily. With two trained Singers, we can get it going, if there's one that's down here." Almost at that moment, Maskar brushed against what had seemed to be a solid wall, discovering quickly that it was little more than a moveable panel, metal, but treated to look like stone. A little tugging at it revealed exactly what they'd been looking for, a small boat sitting out of the water on what seemed to be small logs of metal. The boat would be a tight fit for everyone, but, should it prove sturdy, it would be adequate. It, like the door that had hidden it, was made of metal, but a quick shove into the water proved it buoyant.

Using a grip on the sides to hold it steady, Sihan'el and his father held it in place for the others to board. It became much less troublesome once Maskar was standing near the bow, his hands on the crystal that would power it. Moments later, Vishti and Kialor were helping pull Father up, and then Sihan'el himself, getting them all packed into a boat that likely had only been intended to hold four or five people.

Once they were aboard, Kialor glanced toward the bow, then nodded his head. "That's the direction, and it will get us fairly close, I think. I imagine that some of this actually predates most of what Maskar knew, too. It's like what you've told me about the room in the cave, Sihan'el, someplace where the ancient science of our ancestors merged with the magic that they were gaining through resonant power. Neither had a strength over each other at that point, but the science was fading, and magic beginning to take power."

Sihan'el only vaguely remembered telling Kialor about the near fight he'd had with Maskar, the fight that had been avoided only by the intervention of that strange little woman who had told Maskar that there was something he needed to see. It had made a difference, somehow, coming from her, that there might be something valuable that he didn't have or know yet. Sihan'el had come to realize, since then, that Maskar was extremely devoted to his Dark Lands wife, but there was more to it than appeared. Perhaps Maskar had been truly desperate at the time, trying to find a solution that would enable Evanira to continue living when she might not have been able to. Humans had such short lifespans, he remembered.

The boat started moving, gliding gracefully, without a song needed, not with Maskar's ability with tah'nel. Perhaps, later, he might change places with Father, letting Maskar rest while Father controlled the boat. Singing, or even using the tah'nel, was difficult work, for all that it might not seem that way to most people. Sihan'el had not received full training in that, and realized that, today, he was glad of that fact. It kept him from becoming someone else needed for controlling their passage. That was one responsibility that he didn't want.

Hela seemed to have relaxed, having wet her throat with the water in the canal, for such the river had become, and washed away a little of the dried blood that still covered much of her face and hands. She still hurt, and that was something Sihan'el knew was as much his responsibility to deal with as anyone else's. She noticeably kept her eyes away from where Hrif sat on the edge of the boat. She might still be angry that she'd had to lose her horse, while her nephew still kept his bird. But Sihan'el understood the need for that bird. It could detect things that they might not be able to, and it could move mostly unnoticed once they reached the surface again. It offered them options that the stallion would not have been able to do. That, however, did not deal with the fact that Hela still felt that she'd betrayed someone who trusted her with its life, unwisely. That was something that might never wholly heal.

The boat wasn't fast, but it was faster than walking. Here and there, crystals blinked into awareness, providing more light than they'd had normally. The smell of the water changed, having other things added to it, likely the scents of refuse disposed of casually within the fortress. They were indeed getting closer, he sensed, though he couldn't be certain of where they would show up. It just meant that they would have to be more careful as they got closer. Others might be able to sense the resonant magic, though few had a tah'nel as powerful as Maskar's or Father's. With luck, Sihan'el suspected that they might just stand a chance, from surprise alone. That wasn't counting on the hints that Kialor had made, and Father and the two priestesses were silent on the matter.

Chapter 27

Vishti drew in her breath as the boat moved into a position below what she could sense was a large source of resonant magic. The source was so distinctive, it almost made her head ache with its awareness. And yet, she was nearly certain that it was not aware of her or her companions, not yet. The slip that held the boat was well made stone, with anchoring chains on both sides to hold the boat in place, anchoring chains that had somehow not rusted in this damp environment. Wide steps ascended from the landing, going up in a brightly lit area, an area that seemed to simply respond to their presences. An area that seemed to have been waiting for them.

The area was made of very well fitted stone, not a chisel set to it, it seemed, but shaped by other means. There were crystals everywhere, crystals of all sorts, many of which likely had purposes forgotten even in the Mayisna's own time. There were banks which were very well made, humming with power, and, if she had been in a vengeful mood, she might have tried activating these to decimate the kril'dga above her. But, she discovered, she was not in a vengeful mood, not at all.

She didn't tell Kialor yet, or her father, but she had an idea of what she intended to do, when they reached the heart of their troubles. She could even tell where the Mayisna would be when the time came. But it was not time yet, and they had other things that needed to be dealt with, including those who had caused the Dead. They had retreated, taking the time that the party had rested to hasten back to the fortress. Vishti had no idea how they would deal with that, but destroying those who had raised the Dead would likely not be easy, even with the Mayisna no longer in a state to lead them. There would be those among the great in this place that would resist change, and that change had to be allowed to happen, for everyone's sake.

Maskar moved forward, almost feeling the walls to see the best way to open up these chambers, so that the party could ascend into what amounted to a small city. It was in aspect a city of women, with a few children, but a city none the less. The men were relegated mostly to an area near the docks. They would be primarily non-combatant in this, she hoped, but it was not something to be known. When you had a city full of assassins, anything could happen.

After a few tries, a door opened, sliding neatly into the wall, almost silent in its movement. Whatever machinery was used for it, and Vishti suspected that it was machinery, rather than magic, it still functioned after all these years. It was rather an amazing thing. She smiled and nodded at the dah'ral Singer, then moved up toward the door, only pausing to try to bolster Hela's mental strength with a gentle embrace. For all that the priestess had attempted to remain untouched emotionally, Vishti knew that she needed a lot of help, especially now.

The passage led to a circular stairway, rising up into the darkness, or what would have been darkness, except for the fact that the lighting awakened itself, or one of the Singers had awakened it, as they got near enough to need it. The air was still musty, but breathable, and there were inscriptions here and there in a language that Vishti could not read as she paused to look at it in her ascent. Kialor also paused at those points, taking a moment as if he were memorizing what he'd seen, or perhaps transferring it mentally to the Goddess that Vishti could only vaguely feel at the edges of her awareness. She knew that's what it was, because she'd brushed at the awarenesses of all six gods when she'd handled the Great Music. And, in having become the world to some extent while the Music was being done, she had connected herself with their doings, probably on a deeper level than most of the People would be. There was no way to rescind that connection, only endure it. And it really wasn't a big problem for her, just something she needed to be aware of.

At the top of the stairs was a panel, with both strange knobs on it, and a crystal visibly sitting in one of the glass tubes that were used for such controls. Maskar and Redel were looking at it intently, trying to see what it was that they needed to do to get out and into the main Fortress. Maskar looked at Redel, shaking his head, "That crystal isn't the key, and I have no idea how to read the writing on this device to see how it works."

Kialor moved up next to them, studying what lay before them, but he also didn't seem to have any answers, at least not any that were immediately voiced. Vishti knew that she wasn't really the type of person to be able to make sense of these, but she looked anyhow, trying to see if any of the knowledge she had from what Uncle Telin had given her would offer any understanding at all. She doubted it would, but decided that it was worth attempting, if nothing else.

The symbols on the panel weren't in her language, or even the older form that she and Sihan'el had studied years ago. No, they were much more simple than that, not even picture words like she'd heard that the Toyurasan used. No, they were symbols specifically designed to be easily understood. She wondered why no one else got them.

She pointed to where there was a line with two triangles, one on each side of it. The triangles were on end, with points at the top and bottom, then facing away from each other. "That, I think, is a sign for spreading a door, opening something." She pointed to another, with a strange star-like symbol on it, one that shown heavily with red on the description, "I think that one is dangerous, though I can't really explain it." She moved her fingers through the symbols for another one she could read, but ended up shaking her head, "I don't understand most of it, but those I do. We should use the one with the arrows to get out of here, I think."

Redel looked at her, then at the symbols, and it seemed that something clicked into place in his mind. He pointed to a symbol that looked almost like a scroll, but not quite, and moved the lever above it. Almost instantly, the glass panel behind the machine bank lit up, projecting an image that seemed almost like a very ancient map, one that held several doors and rooms on it, but clearly wasn't the full city. A green star showed up at one point, and a hallway led to a series of rooms from that, with one being noted in a strange gold color, with actual symbols in the oldest form of the language above it.

"Well, that's exactly what we were looking for. We seem to have been in luck," her father laughed, "I think the green star symbol is us, and that gold one is the crystal chamber, where Uncle Telin managed to get into that other place. If this is right, we will have an entrance there that probably hasn't been used in thousands of years. Who knows, we might even find our enemy there, though I wouldn't count on it."

Maskar laughed, "I don't think it will be that easy, Cousin, but it's worth a shot. I think I now know what was meant by crystal room, since I'd not seen it in this life. It's got to be the crystal bank that had once been used to study the Heavens, and the worlds as they connected to this one. It makes sense, too. I only vaguely remember it, because those weren't my studies, but it does make sense that it would have been the place for the magic which would take Mi'la out of this world. Indeed, it's probably almost the only place that could do that. There are special things about that area, the way it interacts with the world's harmonics."

Kialor took the moment while the others were talking to quickly embrace Vishti, gently kissing her on each cheek before on the lips. "Just when I think our luck might have worn out, people do something different and offer us new chances. I think I'm going to have to do a lot to properly reward you later, when we get home, if we do. You've given us much more of a chance than I'd expected."

Vishti beamed under the compliment. This was something she wanted to feel, like she was able to do something right, help someone with something that they weren't able to do alone. It wasn't something that she expected to do, but she was more than willing to work at it when she could. "So, we'll go on down that passage, and come out where the enemy doesn't expect us?"

Redel nodded, "Yes, Vishti, we'll be doing that. We should surprise everyone, since they likely don't realize that we can come in this way. They'll be waiting at the front gate, and we'll be coming at them from behind. And, well, I get a feeling that there's a lot more going on than what we realized. I feel that Railah's moving, already, almost as if, well, it's almost as if I can hear an echo of swordsong, but far enough away, or insulated by this stone, that I can't tell anything more about it. If there's another 'Sword, even a newly called one, we might have a better chance than we expected."

Vishti smiled, hugging her father, then nodded. "Then we should go on. They may need us, with what's likely happening. I doubt that even the previously loyal sisters like having the Dead raised. It would make them more scared. So, maybe they'll help us, at least those who have nothing to gain from our destruction."

Sihan'el's voice echoed that. "I think that many of them will fight. Not many will be agents like your mother, Vishti, but there will be a few of those, too, if they haven't been found out yet."

Vishti didn't wince at the mention of her mother. Indeed, she found that a part of her welcomed the idea of possibly making things right. She didn't know where this change came from, but accepted it. There was no reason not to.

Chapter 28

No matter how much she wanted to focus on her own pain, her own internal suffering, Hela could tell that there was a great deal of destruction going on above her, in the Fortress itself. It surged within her, in a way, a reaction to the forces at play here. As likely the only direct servant of Vythen, she would be attuned to the battle, the hatred and anger, the blood being spilled. She could feel it almost as a source of strength, something to keep her moving even when there wasn't enough food in her body to do so. She realized that it must be worse for Maskar, as he had had no sunlight, and no food. His energies must be very low at this point, and they needed to get someplace where he could take in light, no matter how dangerous it was.

But he made no complaints, likely because he knew how difficult their situation was. Considering his state, and how much he depended on sunlight, Hela decided, at this stage, that her own pains were little more than nuisances. Yes, she would mourn what she'd had to do, and try to exact a blood price upon those who had made it necessary, but she was whole, strong. She would fight, taking command as necessary, but she would also try to aid those who needed it, including a companion she had largely tried to avoid up till now.

She followed Redel as he led the way up the passage that had been indicated, finding that it led to a strange door that seemed stuck, at least immediately. Even as Maskar was pressing at it, Hela could see Vishti concentrating. Then, almost at once, the panel opened, sliding out of the way in almost enough of a rush to leave the dah'ral falling to the ground. Even as he looked around, trying to figure out what happened, Hela shook her head, giggling. "Well, you were expecting machinery. She didn't." Hela pointed to Vishti, who looked quite pleased with herself.

"The tah'nel?" Maskar asked, even as he dusted his clothing off.

Vishti nodded, "It asked me if I needed in, and I told it yes. I can't explain it better than that."

It was a good thing that the room beyond was empty. If it hadn't been, they could have been attacked during that exchange, but, aside from the huge crystal in the middle and a few crystal banks scattered around the sides, there was nothing there, not even a chair to sit in. Hela wondered how this might have looked when Uncle Telin and Aunt Selah had been here. They hadn't told her much about it, only that there was a big crystal, and it had seemed that the Mayisna had been suspended within it, just as in Iera's dreams, with a dagger in one hand, and a cup in the other, a blindfold tied around her head. That had to have been distressing, to have been imprisoned like that, but that thought did not weaken Hela's desire to bring to an end the Mayisna's reign, at the end of her scimitar if possible. It would be blood to answer for her stallion's.

But that was neither here nor there. They needed to get someplace to deal with the dangers here. "We need to find a way to the surface, quickly," Hela commented, pointing to Maskar, whose face had seemed to have lost its usual almost-luminescence. "He's not going to be any help at all unless we can get him where he can recover, at least a bit."

Redel exchanged looks with his son and daughters, then nodded, something having passed between the four that wasn't immediately comprehendible. Then he moved toward the door, causing it to open without a single note crossing his lips. The hall to the right began to rise, and soon there were stairs that Redel ushered them all up. Almost naturally, Sihan'el took the lead, seeming to know what it was that his father had intended. He might not have been at Hela's side in this case, but he was doing what she knew he needed to do. Sometimes he would have to aid the group before aiding her, and this seemed to be one of those times. Even as he reached the hallway ahead, he warbled out a command to hurry, and broke into a jog along a corridor that had bits of light flickering along it, natural light, a sign of the sun above.

There was fighting up ahead, though who was fighting what was less known. Hela could feel the throb of battle, almost as if she were tasting every drop of blood being spilled, every beat of a heart as it tried to recover from the injuries being dealt to it. She'd never felt this way before, but suspected that it had to do with what she'd done, linking Vythen's essence into her people's nature. It could have left her hyperaware of those near her, even if she didn't try to be. But, it could also be a way of the Dread Lord commanding her, urging her to be a part of this destruction, marking it with his name and blessing.

There, the sunlight shone in, access to a balcony, doubtless, above the courtyard, from what Hela could feel of the location of the battle. She could hear Redel moving up behind her, humming in a way to start activating some of his crystals. Those would be almost necessary, offering the team protection while Maskar began to regain enough energy to aid with magical battles. No matter how little Maskar liked to kill, there was a good chance that he would do so today. There would be little he could do to avoid it.

Hela reached the balcony almost at a run. Her scimitar was loose in her left hand, while she held a spell in her right, a coruscating beam of destructive force that she intended to use on her nearest enemy. But what she saw at first was not an enemy. It was a woman, already bloody and injured, with a greatsword in her hands, struggling to recover after having finished off several opponents. That woman seemed to pulse to Hela's sight with a deep red light. Even as the others moved up, Hela shouted to Sai'velk, "Grant her healing, she's on our side."

Redel placed a ward to keep enemies from advancing on where the woman stood, granting her the time to gain such healing as Sai'velk could arrange. His own sword came to hand, drawing a sharp look from the woman below, the woman who seemed to have heard something that no one else did. But Hela was used to that. She'd lived around Sacred Swords for a long time. They had something, swordsong, that identified them to each other. Doubtless the woman had never had a chance to hear that before, and was startled by the way it acknowledged their similar nature.

Redel was moving in that direction, even as Maskar drank in the light of the sun overhead. There was something different, seeing a pair of knights, one newly called, acknowledge each other. Hela could only hear a few of the words, but the ones she did gave her a rather greater respect for her cousin.

"It's good to see another of us, Sister, and that is said with no irony, for your calling makes us allies, brother and sister under Railah's gaze." It was a sign that the knight held no ill will toward the one who might have been his enemy before, perhaps had even been sent to cause harm to those he considered kin, but who was now the best battle partner he could have. Redel had that kind of easy going way, though, that sense that anyone could be a friend, if you approached them right. It might have been almost the only reason Hela had gotten along as well as she had. He hadn't promised any judgment against her, and indeed had treated her with the same sort of respect and consideration she imagined he treated anyone. There seemed to be no difference in status to him.

Hela caught sight of enemies moving closer, those intent upon the two knights on the landing below. She let loose a blast of energy at the first of those enemies, realizing quickly that they would likely be overwhelmed if the group got to the knights in a single knot. Then her attention shifted to those behind the kril'dga. That was much more problematic. Her senses could tell her that those following were the Dead, and she called out, in Trade, "They're running from the Dead. That may be of aid." She kept it in Trade, hoping that perhaps it would not be understood if they were the enemy.

Kialor took a place beside Hela on the balcony, Vishti right behind him, then he seemed to light up, almost as if hope unlooked for had appeared. Then she saw someone else, someone she couldn't see well just appear next to Redel, and moments later disappear, leaving the new knight alone. That didn't stay long, however, as Sihan'el was already moving to help the woman, with Vishti following close behind. Whatever had happened to take Redel away, it seemed not to be a negative, or else she would have heard more from Kialor. Instead, she saw him smile, almost laugh.

"What is going on?"

“That was our distant uncle, there, the Sikal. I imagine that he has a very good plan for what’s going to happen next. He wouldn’t be here if it weren’t to turn the battle in our favor. We just have to find a way to give him and Father a chance to do so.”

Uncle Lisor. That made too much sense, especially that Kialor would know just moments before the Sikal had actually appeared. They both served the same Goddess, and that Goddess was known to make subtle, unexpected plays. What those plays would do with Redel was less understandable, but they doubtless had reason. And Kialor was right. They had to hold the battle for long enough for whatever was necessary to happen.

Chapter 29

Redel caught sight of the newly Chosen knight and moved quickly to stand by her side. Even if she had reasonable skill in the weapon, and she might have that, she was already injured and would need support to stand against the enemies that were coming, and they seemed to be coming quickly. There was something odd, however, about how the kril'dga were running. Something that did not instinctively scream enemy at him. His suspicions were confirmed when he caught a whiff of decay from the direction people were coming at him in. Whether these were potential allies or enemies might not matter much at all for more than a few minutes, he decided.

To his surprise, someone else appeared, someone he hadn't been looking for, and only the descriptions he'd been given before gave him any confidence in. The man was reasonably short, with black hair and a distinctive golden cast to his skin, dressed in clothing that looked almost silver. The man, however, simply appeared out of nowhere next to Redel, grimacing as he looked over the situation.

"Redel, I'm going to need you to trust me. We can stop this part of it, but you're the only one with a chance to. Your new sister in faith doesn't have nearly the experience. I'll get you behind the Dead, and you'll have to let your Goddess act through you. She's already agreed with the council on this. Such behaviors are not to be accepted, at all. And the punishment you'll be wielding against them might make this fight a lot simpler."

"Punishment?" Redel tried to say, just as the scene shifted, his position completely changed from what it had been. It was not unlike how it had happened when Maskar used the old dah'ral transport system, but it was much faster, and without any song being made at all. Nor a use of tah'nel. Just the ability of a sikal to transport him from one place to another, including changing directions he was facing just as quickly.

Railah's will came into Redel's head, in a way just as powerfully as it had when he was channeling her gifts for Kialor to tie into the web that represented his people. There was no need for an answer from Uncle Lisor, because Redel knew instantly what was being done. He'd heard of it being done once, and that it had completely shocked those around at the time it had happened. An interdiction, of the most powerful type. Railah intended to end the Dead in a way that conveyed punishment and displeasure in one neat package. And he was the vessel for it.

Standing in front of him were a trio of kril'dga mages, one of whom he'd actually known in his time here so long ago now. These had to be the ones who were commanding the Dead, those who had summoned them to fight. While killing them would not necessarily lay the Dead to rest, what he had been told to do would, with a guarantee that would display the Goddess' power completely. She'd needed a representative here to do it, and that might be why the Sikal had brought him to this position.

They hadn't noticed him, so he cleared his throat, SkySong loose in his hands. "The Goddess of law, justice, and magic has seen what you have done, and she denies it. Each of you three, those who have called upon those who should rest peacefully, have earned her utmost anger. And the penalty is final, demanded of you without any chance for release. Railah calls for your interdiction. You will possess no magic again, and all of the magic that you have done before will be undone, removed from the patterns of the world. You are helpless, bound, and you will have no further strength to succor you from the righteous judgment of the gods." He found that the words were easier for him, the contact with the Goddess both fuller and clearer than it had been before. Perhaps that was the effect of the change he'd been a part of. Perhaps it was merely that he had come to a greater degree of peace with who he was, and thus, could accept her guidance more easily. It really didn't matter. What mattered was the force that acted through him as he pronounced the mages' doom.

The results rang through the city, all in a matter of heartbeats. The Dead, numbering in multiple score of corpses, fell where they had stood, where they'd been moving. It would be a great deal of effort to remove the bodies, to clean up the city afterward, but that was not for him to concern himself with. Instead, he looked at the women, wondering what further punishment was decreed, since they had done so much ill. Surely Railah did not intend for them to live. The interdiction served to undo their magic, more than anything else. Their punishments would be different.

Then Lisor was stepping out ahead, head held high despite his lack of height. He didn't even draw a weapon, perhaps counting on the confusion as the mages realized that their connection to magic was gone, and spread his hands. "That was only the first part of this. Redel, what speaks Railah regarding their fates?"

The voice of the Goddess echoed in Redel's head. ~Considering the gifts that I have been given by the Serpent Lord, perhaps a fair return, and a just one, would be to deliver these to one of his who was wronged by their actions. Speak that, and it will be done.~

Redel couldn't help a bit of amusement on that. Hela would get more than a fair return for what she had offered up, and from Railah, rather than from Vythen. "Sikal, Railah suggests that these be given into the hands of the priestess Hela of Vythen, who will take on the role of executioner, even as her god serves often to remove the dangers that the Heavens declare."

Lisor didn't contain the laugh that Redel managed to keep in. "More than fitting. You may not have the experience in this, Nephew, but I can say that your Lady has a significant sense of humor, and in this, she seems to have found irony appropriate."

One of the mages had already begun backing away, almost tripping over one of the corpses that had fallen nearby. But then Lisor was at her side, his fingers wrapping around her arm. Where that might not have been the most powerful way to handle her usually, Redel realized suddenly that as the woman tried to pull away from Lisor, she lacked the physical strength to do so. Somehow, in laying the interdiction, Railah had cut the three off from their own natural gifts, the shapeshifting that was theirs by birth, and likely the tah'nel as well. They were no more powerful than a human, and likely less strong, considering that they had counted more upon being able to enhance themselves, rather than physical exertion.

The scene shifted again, and Lisor was holding the magess, with the other two cowering nearby, right in front of where Hela and Kialor stood. Redel was only a few paces further away, on the stairs leading down. He glanced up as Lisor gave the woman he held a little shove, almost forcing her onto her knees. Then Lisor nodded to Redel, who realized he'd have to give his pronouncement again.

"Priestess Hela, Railah gives into your hands the punishment for these three, those who raised the Dead, and caused, indirectly, the need that brought about your stallion's death. They caused a lot more death too, obviously, and you are charged with the duties of your Lord, executioner as the council sees fit."

Hela blinked, looking over the women. Then she glanced further down the stairs, to where Sihan'el stood next to the new knight. "Sacred Sword Redel, if you could exchange places with your son? I intend to make an offer to him." She still had her scimitar in hand, but there was a look on her face that told Redel that this was going to be a decisive move, and one that could well go either way. But it wasn't his duty to intervene. So, instead, Redel quickly darted down the stairs, taking a place in case of further attackers, at the landing.

Redel positioned himself, however, so that he could see what was being done. This was something he needed to know, some measure of Sihan'el that he hadn't gotten yet. There was no doubt what Hela was offering. What would come of it, however, was less certain. She was going to share her revenge, or try to. Whether Sihan'el would take the chance was uncertain, and Redel realized that he couldn't even decide how he felt about either option.

Sihan'el mounted the steps more slowly, clearly having heard enough to realize what was going on himself. Hela threw off a quick spell, binding two of the captives while the third was free. Then she looked at Sihan'el, eyes narrowed as if trying to decide. "Sihan'el, you have suffered much here, including the death of your brother, and perhaps your son. The choice is yours. Will you hold them for their deaths, or would you prefer to wet your blade? They will die regardless, but your answer might have other effects, for the Dread Lord is watching."

Sihan'el took a deep breath, then nodded, "They deserve death, if not for the death of your mount and my kin, then definitely for the disrespect that they have done to the Dead. Perhaps we should share this. Two will die by one of us, and the third by another. Your choice, Lady, as to which you wish."

Hela's mouth split into a wicked grin, "Then I will grant the greater to you, for the price you paid for our safety was higher. I will hold this one, while you kill, and then we will switch as necessary with the others."

Redel realized he'd seen and heard enough. He focused on the approaching kril'dga, kril'dga that realized that there were no more corpses following them, and armed warriors ahead. Those women did the sensible thing, and backed away. If they didn't have to fight, they wouldn't. And that was something that did ease Redel's heart, which was otherwise distressed at the calm discussion of death. He heard the mages cry out, heard them slump into the ground. That wasn't his job to judge. Railah had given the right to Hela, and she'd chosen to share it. They were doing their jobs while his was different. Now, he needed to see if he could find out where the Mayisna had hidden herself, before other problems manifest.

Chapter 30

Sihan'el had not been expecting his wife to share the kills allotted to her. He understood that he might be called to hold them, though with her magic, she probably didn't need that, and if they'd resisted, perhaps it would have been more satisfying to her need for revenge for what she'd had to do. Yet, instead, she offered him the killing blow on two, and had him hold the third still so that she could wet her blade with the woman's blood. Having just slid his blade home, more quickly than perhaps others were expecting, since it was a formal execution, approved, apparently, by the gods that his father and wife worshipped, he realized that he wasn't completely sure how he felt over the entire thing. It wasn't clear, no matter how he turned the matter over in his mind, if he'd gotten any release himself from the revenge offered him, or if it had merely disgusted him. He'd known, from the first, that those women had to die, but making a show of it really wasn't his style, nor did it seem to properly sate Hela. Indeed, she looked more disturbed than he felt by the action.

He'd known that his father had turned away. Father would say nothing about it; Sihan'el knew that already. Of the others, well, Maskar was looking greener than he had been with no sunlight to energize him, the look he'd given when Sai'velk tried to press a piece of dried jerky on him. Kialor merely pursed his lips and looked away. Perhaps the priest understood that this was necessary, even if it was less than pleasant. Sai'velk, of course, was nigh unaffected. She knew this kind of work from before she'd left the Fortress. Even if she served another master now, she knew why the deaths were necessary, and was not even slightly unnerved by their execution.

Evanira was down on the landing, with Father and the new knight and Vishti. Of them all, Vishti might understand his quandary at the moment. Vishti had withheld her hand on occasion, when threats were brought against her. She'd shown that she could understand others' reasoning, even when said reasoning brought her harm. But she'd also been a whirlwind of destruction before. That she wasn't now was largely a result of the other kril'dga staying far out of the reach of the two knights and the warrior women next to them. Evanira was still in her normal shape, not that of a cat, though Sihan'el wondered if the cat might be more appropriate as they started hunting for the source of the problem, and putting down loyal claws as they went. They might not seek out the claws to kill, but if any tried to block their path, they would fall, especially with none of the Dead to protect them.

Sihan'el wiped his blade on the edge of his tunic and moved down the stairs, ignoring the others for the moment. He knew that Hela was watching him. There was clearly some sort of test going on, since she'd mentioned her god's watchful attention on the event, but he wasn't going to wait around for any kind of manifestation that might occur. He had no interest in such things, only in getting things done that they'd come for. He heard boots on the stairs behind him, and was surprised to find that it was Maskar close at hand, rather than Hela, Kialor, or Sai'velk.

"You didn't have to give in to her, you know," the dah'ral commented, clearly indicating Hela. "Even if you've bound yourself to her, and made a promise to aid her in her service to that god she follows, you had a choice as to whether it would be your hand dealing death."

Sihan'el turned, confused, "And what difference would it have made? The women needed to die, and, indeed, it was likely a mercy to them. They lost all of their power, all of their nature as one of our own. They had no way to defend against any who might want to take revenge for their actions, and doubtless there would be many who desired it. The deaths we dealt were quick, and not exceedingly painful. That they were given to Hela to deal, and she shared them with me, means nothing overall. Death is a necessary part of life. With the exception of you, perhaps, everyone ends up killing to live. All of our food is things that are dead, whether plants or flesh. There is no life without death. And dealing it is occasionally necessary. It may not be pleasant, but why should I shirk an unpleasant duty if it needs to be done? Indeed, why are you so disturbed that I did so?"

Kialor's voice was faint behind Maskar. "Whether you like it or not, Maskar, he may have just bested you. He might not be a follower of any of the faiths, but he just almost word for word quoted how Jirel's followers feel about death, and life. How that turns out to affect things later, I can't say, but his points are perfectly valid."

Sihan'el had not expected the priest to come to his aid. Nor had he expected to be complimented by Kialor. It was a weird feeling, especially as, though Kialor had been helpful on much of the trek out here, he'd never seemed to really like Sihan'el much. Indeed, as closely as Kialor and Maskar worked on things, it would have made more sense to back up the dah'ral.

Maskar snorted, "I was hoping to help keep him out of the web of deception that the council spins. I'd had higher hopes for him, simply because he's managed to keep out of their grasp so long. But to do the work for one, directly, well, it won't be easy to escape that control again."

Sihan'el laughed, "As if you weren't doing their will, or something to their benefits, with that Music you designed. You're no better than me there. And dealing death doesn't make you less of a person, or even less of a person worthy of respect. I wouldn't even say that enjoying something like that, the end of the reign of terror someone had over others, is wrong in and of itself. But you should know something. Much as I am pleased that they have been stopped, and will never trouble this place again, I took no joy in it, only an acknowledgement that those are enemies I will never have to fight again."

Sihan'el reached the landing where the others were waiting. He got a curt nod from his father, all the acknowledgment he expected. "That's perhaps the best way to look at it. When we ease an enemy into death, Son, that's exactly what we're doing, making sure that they are enemies we won't have to fight again, enemies who won't hurt anyone else in this life. I can agree with that, though I would have perhaps disliked the method in this case a bit more."

Hela fell into step right behind Sihan'el, and he knew that she was feeling much the same way. Perhaps it was something that made her more real, less of the imperious priestess she liked to present to the world. That was useful for control, and he was more than willing to allow her that control, but he knew the truth. She regretted the necessity, even as she fulfilled promises he knew she'd made the dying beast yesterday. She had a conscience, but he'd known that already, even if she herself wasn't really aware of it.

Vishti spoke up, where she'd been silent before, and gestured toward a dense cluster of buildings up the path from where these stairs ended. "We must go there. I think that the others will not bother us, not unless we delay too much. The Great Mother is weakened, unable to command well right now. The magic has left her without close command of those she thought were hers. We must hurry, though, before she realizes that she has other means at her disposal."

Sihan'el touched her arm, "You know where the enemy is?"

"I have known, since we got here. We had to deal with other things first. We would be weaker against her if the Dead were still at our backs." Her words were entirely pragmatic, calm and peaceful. Sihan'el wondered why Vishti sounded so centered, so unconcerned about other dangers, or about the hatred she should have for the one who had ordered her tortured almost to death. He'd seen her when she was in pain from the revelation of why her mother betrayed her. Surely this would be worse, because the Mayisna was the one who had ordered those tortures, commanded them intentionally.

Father didn't question her. He merely glanced at his new ally, and warbled off a few questions, "Are you able to help restore order out here? We have things we need to do, but it would be best if fewer of the Sisters here were hurt. They may have been following orders, but I doubt they understood the wrongness of what they were asked to do."

The new knight glanced over the scene and nodded. "There are others, not like me, but others who are working in this. We will calm the place, make sure that those who are not wishing attack are led to safety. We will also do what we can for the corpses. They should be treated with more honor."

That was a feeling that Sihan'el could understand. Even if this new knight had no idea of what she'd just been claimed by, she understood that there were some things that were important. Showing more respect for the dead was a part of that, as was making sure that those who were not willingly a part of the battle were kept safe. Sihan'el hadn't really thought about that until Father had mentioned it at the keep. But yes, the innocent should be safe, if possible.

Redel glanced at Vishti, then gestured to her. "As you know how to find her, lead on. I doubt I have to do much to pull you out of the way if there's trouble, despite what your husband might think."

Vishti seemed to giggle, but it was a clean one, not one caused by pain and wound-illness. “I think that there won’t be much for us to face, Father.” Those words caused Sihan’el worry, though he didn’t know why.

Chapter 31

Vishti led the party through the streets, streets that seemed to empty ahead of them. She wasn't sure, but suspected that the claws here were being guided away by the Rhi'na'n who had hidden in plain sight, those who had, like her mother, risked themselves by staying within reach, just with their identities hidden. It would have to have been a very dangerous way of life, but perhaps better, in some ways, than living out in the wilderness. It was really a big question of whether the risks were worth the advantages of staying within what amounted to a city.

She knew that her father was watching her, trying to see how far he could trust what she would be doing. He had reasons to be cautious, since there had been times when her mind was not completely her own. She imagined he might think that too, when she did what she needed to do. But she was fairly certain that even if Father doubted her reasoning, Kialor would understand. She still wasn't entirely sure how she would do this, but had this sense that she would understand fully when it was necessary. She could almost see the other place, the place where the Mayisna had been bound for so long. She just needed to be able to access it. And she was almost certain that Maskar's words were incorrect earlier. It could be accessed from anywhere. It just might require certain places for people to access it if they didn't understand how it lay over and through everything. That was what she could sense now, how it meshed with the world itself.

Kialor seemed to almost struggle to keep up with her. Perhaps it was because he'd been doing so much for so long. She wasn't sure. But he wasn't going to let her get away from him. If that's what was meant by what he considered love, that was something she hoped to keep for a long time. She liked how he stayed with her, made her feel safe. He'd always wanted to do that, she'd noticed. It reminded her a lot of his grandfather, Caldor. The older man had a lot of that quality, protective in just the right way.

"Are you ready for this?" her husband asked, between gasps he was making to keep moving. His wind didn't sound as good, though he didn't seem to have any injuries that she'd noticed. She wasn't sure why he was so out of breath. All she knew was that he seemed weaker than she was right now. But then, her strength was that of the earth, in a real way. She was falling more and more into that nature she'd held during the Great Music.

Vishti paused for just a moment, turning to smile at him. "I remember that vision I had, on the cliffs. I know what I need to do." She didn't explain further, but started off again, trusting that neither he nor Father would stay more than a few paces back. The others might.

She'd seen Sihan'el's face after he'd killed those mages. She'd seen his inherent distaste for what he'd done. In a way, that had decided her, if there had been any doubts left at that time. He hadn't enjoyed harming those who had raised those he knew personally, had sent them against her family and the Rhi'na'n. Neither had Hela enjoyed her kill, despite the fact that they had been given to her for revenge, a blood price, as such. No, if there had been any doubts about the fact that revenge wasn't in her nature, it had vanished when she'd seen how empty such victories were. It made her very glad that she hadn't gone to kill her mother when she could have.

That building on the right, the one with resonant wards, that was where she was going. A glance at Father had those wards deactivated, for they were simple enough. She just had little control over the resonant magics herself. They could flow through her, but she really was more like a lens that focused the energies, rather than capable of handling them herself. She gestured at the doors, and moved toward them. Especially as, almost as soon as the wards had dropped, she could hear something else, a cry of pain and anguish.

Maskar was looking ahead, and the doors appeared to open of their own will. Sihan'el's fire began to lance at one guard who moved to rush out at them. The woman was hit quickly, and fell, dropping to the ground to extinguish the flames. The other standing at the doorway stood back, clearly realizing that she was just as much in danger as her companion had been, and that trying to fight here might be worthless.

Vishti took the stairs into the building quickly, almost running. Then she realized what she'd heard, and knew a desperation that she hadn't expected to feel. On the ground, at the foot of a dais, lay her mother, wounds in several places, and blood pooling around her. Some of those wounds had been made over a period of time. Others were fresh, including one that could well prove fatal quickly. That had been delivered by the woman at the top of the dais, a woman with hair like smoke, and eyes that blazed with ire. That woman spoke out, with a voice that conveyed an ego far too great for that body. "I dealt with one traitor, and now others come for their rewards."

Vishti's throat caught with pain, realizing that her mother must have attempted to end this war herself, and most likely had been revealed before she could strike by the touch on Evanira's mind. She was overwhelmed with compassion, with a desire to see her mother strong again. And there was only one way to do that, since Sai'velk was likely not nearly powerful enough to save her.

Indeed, that was what her sister said, even as she caught sight of the wounded woman at the foot of the dais. She probably didn't even know who it was, only that it was an ally of sorts to them. "I can do nothing for her. The wounds are too great."

Vishti clinched her teeth, words barely managing to come out, "Not for me. And this will end now." She stepped past her father, who had come to try to shield her, and moved to a spot nearly halfway between the two, the Great Mother and her mother. Then, deliberately, she changed things, pulling all three out of the reality that they knew, into something else.

The Mayisna knew this place, and doubtless feared it. She had never understood what had been done to her. She had no idea how to control the nature of what was around her. It meant that Vishti could safely turn her attention first to her mother. "Mother," she managed, trying not to become overwhelmed herself, though not by the power around her, but by the pain inside her. "Relax, and you'll be healed. I know how to do this."

It was simple, amazingly simple. She merely had to reach for the time before those injuries, indeed the time after Mother had left the keep that they'd raided. It was almost like pulling a piece of yarn from a skein and going to a specific point and twisting. Sah'lev'da'kril changed, but was left poised at that moment, not really aware of what was happening, just real in that reality. It left Vishti the means to deal with the Mayisna.

"Mi'la," she tried the name out with her mouth, "I know why you hurt, why you're scared. I haven't come to imprison you again, to make you hurt. Not even because of the hurt you'd given me. No, I want to give you something better, something easier to deal with. I know that you feel alone, like the only people you ever trusted were torn from you, especially your father. You don't know it, not yet, but you're the reason he disappeared. When you were here, you called him, and you called him through time. He ended up neither here nor there, just absent. And we're going to correct this, you and I. I need you to call him again. Ask him to come to you."

The Mayisna was nearly hysterical, terrified, but, in a way, that made it easier to get her to do what Vishti needed her to. It brought her back to the mental state of a child, terrified and helpless. In that state, she could call to her father, and be answered. Vishti knew it instinctively. Just as she somehow knew that the father had indeed merely been taken, trying to find his little girl.

A man appeared out of the mists, someone clearly of the people, though his coloration could match that of humans. There was just something about him that she knew he was ke'dahr, even if he had little enough of the People's gifts. He looked perplexed, like he was looking for something, only to find Mi'la, a woman grown, sobbing at his feet in moments. She could make no clear words, only cried helplessly. That, amusingly, made things easier for what Vishti would do.

"Friend, that is your daughter, but she was changed, taken to this place that cannot be, and was brought to do much ill. I do not blame her for that, because the ill she did she did because of the use she was put to, the tortures of mind, if not body, that she faced. I've asked her to call you here so that we can give her a second chance."

“That is Mi’la, my daughter?” The man sounded incredulous, then looked around at what he could see, which seemed like a swarm of colors and fading objects. Vishti decided not to give him any time to question much. She moved herself next to Mi’la, and placed her hand on the woman’s shoulders, concentrating. Much as she had done with her mother, she did with Mi’la, but taking her much further, back to where none of this would have happened. In moments, it was an infant floating within her reach.

“That is Mi’la, and you are needed now. No one will take her from you, not this time. But we must return, for this place will undo what I have done if we spend much time here. Take her up, hold her, and I will bring her to where she was, before. It is not where you were before, but there are reasons, including the world we must save.”

Even as the man picked up the infant, wrapped her tightly in the blanket that had replaced Mi’la’s robes when the transition occurred, Vishti focused on her mother a moment, then sent all of them, Mi’la, her father, Sah’lev’da’kril, and Vishti herself, back into that room with the dais. For the world that they’d left, no time would have passed, and only the changes would be noticed, instantly.

Chapter 32

Kialor rushed for Vishti, having seen her vanish, then reappear elsewhere. It had only been seconds, but it startled him, and he was worried, especially at realizing who it had been on the ground when she'd vanished. He paused only a few feet from her, taking in the scene, before moving to crush her in his arms, planting kisses on both cheeks. He had only paused to make sure that the Mayisna, who was likely the one who inflicted the wounds on Sah'lev'da'kril, was not there, or at least not in any way he could understand. He wasn't concerned about anything at that moment except that she was safe.

He paused, releasing her slightly, when he heard a laugh from the man that had appeared behind Vishti. The laugh was perhaps a little off from a trill, but still decidedly from one of the People. Then the comments came, "I can see that someone cares for you as much as you understood that I care for her, Miss, whoever you are."

Kialor didn't let go of Vishti, but moved to where he could see the man, and what he was holding, a little better. "I do have reason to worry over her, Sir. I don't know who you are, but I imagine that what just happened was my wife's doing, rather than yours, isn't it?"

Maskar spoke up from elsewhere in the room. "He's someone I didn't expect to see again, honestly, ever. And I didn't see him last in this life. My greetings, Rah'let'vel. Now I think I know what to make of the image that was left, when you'd vanished, back in the height of our people's hubris."

The man looked confused. "You know who I am, but I'm less knowledgeable about your identity, or where we are. There were things the woman said about my daughter, things she'd done, that left me with a sense that time has passed, though I have no idea how."

Kialor blinked, then looked closely at the baby in the man's arms. He wasn't sure how it was, but that was the woman who'd been threatening them only minutes before. That was the Mayisna, but now an infant. It would have been impossible for anyone but Glea, unless, well, Vishti had said some things that had made no sense. Now they did. She'd been someplace that Uncle Telin had been, but been able to do something else with it. Time and space meant nothing, and thus, much to everyone's surprise, the Mayisna was an infant, likely with no memory of her prior life, and that man, well, it could be her missing father.

But Vishti was pushing herself out of his arms, moving in the opposite direction of the man who carried the infant. Almost before Kialor could realize what she was doing, she was kneeling next to Sah'lev'da'kril's fallen form, gently shaking her, as if to wake her from a bad dream. "Mother?"

The Rhi'na'n agent seemed shocked. Her eyes widened, and she looked around the room in utter confusion. Her clothes were different too, looking not unlike what she'd been wearing during the raid on the keep. In fact, those seemed to be the very ones. Sah'lev'da'kril shook, unable to form words for a long moment. When she did manage a few, they indicated how startled she was. "You name me that? After…" She didn't manage anything else, being enveloped in Vishti's arms, hauled to her feet. Thankfully Redel had come up quickly, his sword sheathed, and helped to brace her until she could understand what just happened.

The words that came from Vishti's mouth were simple, and something that Kialor realized that no one here expected from her. "Mother, I understand, and I forgive. I brought you back, because you needed to hear that."

Father laughed, a hearty guffaw, even as he steadied Sah'lev'da'kril's stance. "It seems that she's willing to surprise everyone, and that is not necessarily a bad thing. I'm not sure who is most to be praised for that, or if a lot of this came to her naturally, but she's indeed worthy of pride. And, where I wasn't entirely sure how much I wanted to trust you, I can't refuse to do so after her show of loyalty. I can't imagine loyalty like that ever truly being misplaced."

Kialor watched as Sah'lev'da'kril almost collapsed into Vishti's arms, weeping with the shocks she was experiencing. And she wasn't alone for very long, as Sihan'el was also there, taking his release from the care of someone he'd clearly respected for a long time, and the sister that, at one time, he thought would never forgive him. It was a hug that lasted several heartbeats, until a call from behind them brought everyone to their senses.

"Brother," the speaker could be no other than the newly called knight, "there is something strange. The spirits have taken most of the corpses, but two they have placed in places of honor outside."

Kialor moved quickly. If there were faedh here, there was likely a very good reason for it. He knew, too, that there was still a price that hung over him, though he didn't know if now would be the time. He was the one who had experience speaking with the nature spirits. He would likely be involved in whatever they were doing. He let the others follow, more slowly, except for Father, who was right at his side. But what he found outside the building was almost enough to make him lose his voice, waiting for the others to catch up.

Two biers lay in the road, made of all sorts of vegetation, and on one of them rested the corpse of a red-haired man, one with features that looked familiar. The other was smaller, holding a boy of perhaps five or six summers, likewise dead, with hair of an almost emerald green. Between the biers stood a translucent figure of a woman, her hands gesturing to the two corpses beside her.

Vishti cried out behind him, and he could hear Sihan'el gasp and then fall to the ground. That told Kialor who the dead bodies belonged to, better than anything else would have. He didn't need Sihan'el's moan stating that one was his brother Vedask, and the other his son Vashk. That kind of heart-wrenching sound made all too much sense. In the middle of all of the joy of seeing Vishti's forgiveness of her mother, there was also a darker tone of pain, of deepest loss.

Kialor didn't hesitate, moved toward the faedh woman, the air spirit, and knelt before her, "It's time for my choice, isn't it?" He hardly needed the confirmation. At her feet sat the small pot he'd made, not too long ago, still stained a bit by the addition of his blood.

She smiled down at him, "You knew that a choice would be offered. Now you know the price of it. That choice is yours, and yours alone. One to save, one life to restore from death. No other may make it for you, though you can hear from others, if you wish."

He shook his head, picking up the jar. "I know what I must do, High One. I know which life is more important now. Father never knew Vedask, and Vishti and Sihan'el have grown used to that loss. It is better that Vashk be saved, so that his father has a chance to be in his life."

He could see Redel nod as he took the pot and moved toward the child's bier. Sihan'el seemed not to have heard anything, such was the depth of his sorrow. Kialor nudged him, speaking softly. "Let me do something for you, Brother. I can do something, this once, to make a real difference." Even as Sihan'el instinctively retreated from the nudge, Kialor knelt next to the bier, taking the pot and placing it on the boy's chest. It was almost as if it was beginning to melt, for it flowed into the child's body, glowing with an array of colors, soaking into the wounds and healing them. It wasn't instant, but didn't take long, and suddenly the child's chest rose, and there was a cough, then a squeal, as the boy raised his hand to wipe at an eye.

Sihan'el's arms flew around Vashk's form, picking him up and crushing him to his own chest. There were sobs, silent but powerful, that left Sihan'el unable to do anything for a long moment. Even as Kialor backed up, trying to give Sihan'el more room for comfort, and perhaps room for Hela to come up beside him, Kialor heard the faedh speak again.

"Child, your heart is great, perhaps great enough for another miracle, when one considers that you gave your gift to one who you have disliked in many ways. Will you be willing to give another, of a different kind? The question must be played also to the one who granted forgiveness and mercy where it was unexpected. This one who remains dead could be brought to rebirth faster. Would you do that, you and your wife? His rebirth would be through you. No memories of who he was, but offering a chance that he didn't have in the life he gave up."

Kialor looked at Vishti, realizing what it was that the faedh was asking him. "Vishti, you'll be the one in pain from this, both pain from his loss, and pain from his rebirth. Is this something you want to do, become a mother to the spirit of your brother?"

Vishti hardly hesitated, wrapping him in her arms. "I think that would mean other types of work between us, since it wouldn't be instant. If you're willing to put that effort into it, I'll gladly bear him. Mostly because I enjoy more than merely being held by you."

Kialor coughed, even as Father laughed from the background. "I can think of no couple I would prefer to raise a child who bears the spirit of a son I couldn't raise. I have little doubt that you'll be more than adequate for the job, both of you. Vishti has shown that she can forgive even the worst of pains, and you, Kialor, are one who I would have been extremely proud to have as my own son. I know your father thinks much the same, especially after what he saw while he was out here."

Kialor blushed, and glanced back over to where the faedh stood. “I believe that is decided, High One. Vishti and I will bring him to rebirth, with the blessing you have offered us here.”

The air spirit laughed, jubilant chiming through the air. “Then it is done, and the work for that shall be left to you.” Moments later, she vanished, leaving the group staring at now empty biers.

Chapter 33

There were no words for how Sihan'el felt about what had been done for him. He was overwhelmed, first by what Vishti had done, in saving her mother, someone that Sihan'el still felt positive feelings for, and then what Kialor had done with the corpse of Vashk, giving the boy life again. It was almost too much to process, but Sihan'el knew that his first focus needed to be on his son. Especially with the Sisters here having gotten the city back in hand, he needed to make the most of the gift he'd been given. He kept warbling softly to the boy, telling him that he would be going home soon, to a new home, and that Hela would be Vashk's new mother. That last was important, especially as the golden-haired priestess was never far away.

There was another man nearby too, caring for a much smaller child. It only struck Sihan'el, after the shock of having Vashk in his arms again began to fade, who this man must be. Maskar had named him, and the man kept calling the infant in his arms Mi'la. While it didn't make much sense to Sihan'el, he knew that this had to be the Mayisna's father, and that the Mayisna herself had to have been changed into this infant. It gave him a strange ability to communicate, finally.

"She's not as fussy as I would have expected," Sihan'el started, trying to find something simple and safe to say, as the man received the child back from the care of one of the kril'dga who had taken over feeding duties. That was rather needful, as the child seemed far too young to eat normal foods, though she could eat a little bit of roots that had been mashed to a pulp. It just wasn't good for her whole diet.

The man glanced over to him, "She wasn't all that fussy before, when she'd been a baby the first time. Usually very calm. She's fussier now, but I think that may be because the woman who helped us told me that she'd been locked in a place that frightened her for more time than any of us could imagine. Maybe, though she hopes that's not the case, some memory of that place lingers in her mind."

"That woman would be my sister Vishti. I don't know how she did what she did, but I'm grateful. Because she managed to find forgiveness in her heart for someone else I respect, even though there is little more than respect and kind feelings anymore between myself and Sah'lev'da. If it helps, my name is Sihan'el, and the man in armor that you'd seen handling the organization here is my father, Redel. I have another sister here, too, and I think she's been watching you, though she's been largely afraid to say much at all here. She had to flee this place, years ago, because of her mother. She isn't sure yet whether her mother lives or not. And that's good enough cause for worry."

The man smiled softly, "You know who my daughter is, doubtless, Mi'la. I am Rah'let'vel, since you gave me your name. I feel strange here, almost overwhelmed. I'm not sure how well I will be able to raise her in this place, because of the deference people seem to treat me and her with."

At that point, another voice interrupted, a highly musical one, for Maskar was clearly filled with enough emotion that his past as a true Singer showed in his voice. "If we can find an easy way back home, I'd suggest you come with us. We have horses, but they're more than a day away, and Hela had had to lose hers, which means fewer, though there are doubtless a few here to substitute. Still, I'd prefer to avoid crossing into the Steppe, and I'm pretty sure that I, at least, would have a cool welcome in Toyurasi. They were rather badly affected by my last journey there."

"You are the one who remembered me, but have said little about yourself. I don't understand," Rah'let'vel spoke, shifting Mi'la in his arms.

Maskar shrugged, "My name then wouldn't give you any comfort, though it was my twin who harmed you both, unintentionally. She regrets that, I know, though she won't know that you've somehow returned, not until we get to Sharlan. She's seen what happened after we failed, and others took over your daughter's education, and forced her to something that was a disaster."

Maskar sighed, seeming to look into the distance, but his manner changed, even as a pair of footsteps caught his attention. Sihan'el looked up to see Sai'velk, and Evanira. That the two were walking together probably meant that Evanira had fully recovered from the manipulation that had been done to her, perhaps because it was clear now that Maskar hadn't been the cause of Mi'la's loneliness, at least not directly. With Rah'let'vel having returned, it meant that some of what was thought of the past was not quite true, at least not in the way most people thought of things.

Evanira gave Sai'velk a slight shove, "You are the one who was asking, Miss, so now is your opportunity." Sihan'el had no idea what was being meant by that, but it had something to do with Sai'velk, and one of the three who had been standing here, himself, Maskar, or Rah'let'vel.

Sai'velk looked down, and her body and hair seemed to cycle through colors. Embarrassment? And of that level? Her voice was hesitant as she addressed not Maskar or Sihan'el, but Rah'let'vel. "The one that I serve, the Phoenix, has an interest in this new chance that the girl, she who was Great Mother to our people, is given. But his interest is perhaps less than my own, and not quite in the same direction." Her words were almost stammered at the last, and Sihan'el nearly laughed at this. Sai'velk had seemed focused before on the elvare who had rescued both Sihan'el and his sister, and yet, now her attention was very much elsewhere, to the point that the well-trained, self-contained priestess was unable to speak clearly.

Sihan'el settled Vashk on the seat beside him, then glanced at Rah'let'vel, "I think you might have found good reason to leave, if you're interested in it. I don't know my sister that well, but I find it highly amusing that she seems to be unable to speak clearly on the matter. At the very least, you should try to get her to speak more, so that you can hear her out."

The man laughed, tilting his head to study Sai'velk, in her robes of gold and red. "I don't know anything of this Phoenix you speak of, but I do know that I've seen uncommon generosity and mercy from your sister, who I assume is younger. Miss, though I don't know your name, I think it might be pleasant, at least for now, to company someone who seems to think well of me. I can't say what will happen in the future, especially as my now is very strange, but you don't need to feel so frightened of me."

She looked up hesitantly, seeming still half-afraid, then advanced a few steps closer. "My name is Sai'velk, and you will likely learn much more of the gods, soon. They have come to our world since your time, save Jirel, who was not worshipped, as such, by the People. But they care for the world, trying to aid us in making all better."

A warm rumble came from the other direction, and Sihan'el looked up to see the rest of the group, Vishti, Kialor, Hela, and Father, as well as someone else, someone who Father looked decidedly uncomfortable around. That man wore robes in a color not unlike Hela's, though perhaps more vivid, seeming to sparkle as he moved. His hair held just a hint of red to its gold, and he carried himself with a confidence that left Hela's usual appearance sorely lacking. There was just something about him that defied understanding.

Redel spoke softly, "A way home has been arranged, once something is done. I believe I heard our newest guest mention that he might appreciate going where his daughter might not be such a spectacle. That can be arranged, easily, though the languages there must be given to you. I know that too can be arranged easily. Sai'velk probably got them from Kialor, when he was gathering other information from her. But, as I said, there is something else that must be done." He stepped out of the path, letting the man in black and viridian move very lightly toward Sihan'el. It was only then that Sihan'el realized this was an elvare, though there was much more of a sense of power to him than had been in the other elvari that Sihan'el had met.

"Thy mettle was tested, Child, in many ways, and I have reason to be pleased with what I saw. The question is whether thou will accept an offer made for thee. Though killing in cold blood clearly displeases thee, thou understand where it may be necessary, and show a respect for life, even while dealing death. Will thou take service, not quite the same as thy mate, my granddaughter here? A spot could be had for thee among mine, a servant who could act at need, and who might train those who have need to act on my behalf."

It took Sihan'el a long moment to realize who he was talking to. The fact that Hela was studiously avoiding his gaze told him a lot of that. Her eyes looked away, and she seemed almost as if she'd been lessoned in something unpleasant. Though the god, for god it was, had hinted not a word of remonstrance when he had described her as his granddaughter. Which, if Sihan'el was reading it right, made he himself the god's grandson, probably distantly.

"I don't know how I could serve you, Lord," Sihan'el realized that formal politeness might be necessary here, since this being could kill him with little more than a thought. Especially with either the sword or the strange serpent's fang hanging from his belt. "I know that Hela chose to do so, but I have little knowledge of my own worth here."

"If thou accept, thou will learn such a place. Thy training here would aid thee, greatly, I think. Though it would not put thee at the beck and call of another merely out of whim."

That statement was tempting. As was the idea that there might be a place for him. He coughed a moment, then lowered his head, "If you want me, despite my faults and weaknesses, Lord, I'm not going to argue with you. You made it possible for me to get something I greatly value, and that at least puts me in your debt."

The god smiled, but not a wicked smile, not one of exultation at all, merely one of acceptance. "Then come, Grandson, and be welcome among mine. Thou will gain the knowledge thou need, soon, but perhaps it is time to return all of thee home. The beasts that are left will be returned, by the faedh who guide them. And another reward awaits my granddaughter when she arrives."

Sihan'el could hardly recognize what was happening before he found himself standing in the dirt, next to the fountain near what he believed he'd been told was a college for bards. The rest of the group was there, excepting the god. It took Sihan'el a moment to verify that Vashk was with him, then he picked the boy up and carried him over to hug Hela. This was now home.

Chapter 34

Hela recognized where they were almost instantly. She should, she'd grown up here, and spent a lot of time in the college at hand, a result of Father teaching there occasionally, and his insistence that she and Iera learned at least a little of the resonant magic that was so much of his life, and Mother's. She knew that it wouldn't take more than a moment before several of the elder members of the family were alerted, though it was far earlier here than she would have imagined, since it was near midday where they had been. She'd remembered that effect with their travel through the dah'ral transport. So, perhaps her father, at least, would be out at the cottage still.

It wasn't a surprise when she saw her Uncle Telin, and then Aunt Selah, appear, completely out of nowhere. Her uncle raised his voice, calling out a few sharp notes that doubtless would bring Grandfather here. And it was Grandfather, and her own father, who didn't seem to be here, who she'd have the hardest time dealing with. It would likely require more of a headache, especially with the fact that she would be going nowhere alone, certainly not after her Lord had made such a show with Sihan'el. And that Sihan'el had accepted, well, that was a bonus in her eyes.

Grandfather wasn't far, and was in armor, so likely just out of a practice, when he appeared, but Telin was going among them, reaching out to tousle the emerald-hair of the boy that Sihan'el was holding, a boy that Hela was still hesitant to call her son, though Sihan'el seemed to want that from her. And Aunt Selah was going to where Rah'let'vel was holding Mi'la, quickly rattling through a couple of languages in order to make sure that he didn't speak Trade. Indeed, by this time, Trade sounded strange to Hela herself. She realized that Vythen had been speaking in a way that crossed languages, when he'd spoken, for he could not make the sounds for the Old Tongue without that. He'd merely used a magic that made himself understood by all.

It was amusing, realizing that Grandfather could not dominate a setting with Redel, even less than he could when Uncle Jalak was present. And it seemed almost strange when Sihan'el straightened himself up to his full height, drawing attention to himself as the old knight came through, greeting those he could easily, and letting Selah handle those whose Trade was poor or non-existent. Sihan'el raised a hand, signing for Arandel to pause, then gestured to Hela. So, he was willing to force the point now. Perhaps that was for the best, since Redel was here to help out if there was any difficulty with the newly formed marriage.

"Grandfather," Sihan'el clearly was trying to be as respectful as he could. "There are things that must be said, now, before they become a problem. While we were in the east, Hela and I found a bond between us, and, with the help of her nephew, formalized that. Thanks to Kialor, my son lives, when he would not have otherwise, and Hela has agreed that he is to be ours, rather than merely mine. But I will not be separated from my wife, regardless of where I may be taken to stay while I learn my true place here."

That startled Grandfather, almost enough to make him reach for his sword. But Uncle Telin stepped up immediately, a faint smile on his face. "Not exactly the ending of the game I'd seen before, but a worthy ending, I think, regardless. It makes something Ranor had mentioned to me make more sense now. Father, I will take them, and the child, into my house, for now, until better can be arranged." There was an edge to Telin's voice, almost like he was daring Grandfather to object. It was a tone that Hela herself had used with her father on occasion, but it seemed almost out of place in Uncle Telin, though Grandfather did not seem so surprised by that as he had by the statements that Sihan'el had made.

Grandfather coughed for a moment, then nodded, "Well, it's quite a surprise, to have another Calasti marriage to accept, and a youngster here, who I will welcome as another grandson. And to hear that respect from you, young man," he indicated Sihan'el, "tells me that perhaps there were a lot of misjudgments along the way, misjudgments we'll have to take some time to correct. Your son?"

"His name is Vashk, though he doesn't speak anything but the Old Tongue yet." Sihan'el glanced at Uncle Telin, "Ranor spoke of something?"

"Only that you would likely be needing some privacy when you returned, nothing more than that. I'm not going to ask anything more than that, though I won't forbid you from explaining if you ever feel you must. I know enough of Hela to imagine that anyone who could manage to convince her to settle down probably has an interesting story, but one that should be shared carefully."

Hela couldn't help but blush, but was quickly saved from that by Redel. "We have a few things that need to be done. Master Rah'let'vel and his daughter will need a place to stay. I can probably stay with Father until I can get back to Chralis, but I have another child I met there, Sai'velk of the Risen One, who proved to be quite helpful for now. I know you have the greatest room, Grandfather, and you would likely need to care for them both at this time, until a better solution can be offered. I doubt Sai'velk would be comfortable in the temple dormitories at the moment, as she has never yet dealt with any priests of her own order. Her calling was rather unique."

Telin pulled Hela aside, and glanced at Sihan'el, "Let's get this taken care of as quickly as possible, before Father starts questioning things. If you think you can handle the stomach churning, I can get you to my brother's cottage quickly enough, though perhaps I should carry the child, since I won't be as affected by the transition. I think it best to deal with this, and then get you both settled in. Whatever you've been through, you'll still need time to recover, doubtless. I intend to make sure that you get that."

Sihan'el looked confused, but handed Vashk over, hesitantly. Almost instantly they were in the middle of Hela's father's house, with both Hela and Sihan'el clutching at their stomachs. It seemed that it bothered Vashk less, though he still showed some distress, warbling out in a language that at least everyone here could understand, even if Syal couldn't speak. Hela got her stomach under control first, softly calling to Vashk to relax, that they were safe.

Maran looked up from where he had just been finishing up his breakfast. He seemed less distressed by the appearance, indeed, willing to stand up and give Hela her expected hug. "I see my wayward daughter has managed to make it home again."

Telin set Vashk down on the floor and held up a hand, "Brother, patience. There are things you must know. Since I suspect that your grandson was just as tight-lipped with you as with everyone else, I imagine this will startle you. But Hela seems to have acceded to a bond that was at least somewhat of a surprise. Redel's son is now as much your responsibility as his father's, though both of them, and the little tyke here, will be staying with Selah and I for the nonce."

Father looked between her and her husband with confusion for a moment, then with a look of distaste. "Bed-bond, I assume?"

Sihan'el seemed to take a moment to decide what to do, then bowed to Father. "Ranor bound Hela and myself together, formally. It was a bed-bond before that, but we chose more, deciding that we worked very well together. And I intend to make sure that Hela lacks for nothing that I can provide, as time goes forward. She accepted my son, Vashk, for which I will be very grateful."

Father was clearly uncomfortable, but looked about to speak up, before another voice caught him off-guard. "Hela accepted his claim. You may ask for a service, but cannot stop that claim." It was Mother's voice, seeming to see below the surface. And enough below the surface that Hela herself couldn't help but blush.

Sihan'el laughed, wrapping an arm around Hela, "Our claims are mutual, and I am amenable to whatever you demand for the privileges I've had in her company. Hela gave me chances that I couldn't have gotten anywhere else, and I intend to prove myself worthy of that."

Father finally caught his words, and moved to hug Hela, then Sihan'el, then picked up Vashk, warbling a quiet greeting to the little boy before switching back to Trade. "Well, it's not what I'd expected, but perhaps better than I'd hoped for. I welcome you further into my family, Sihan'el, and get the feeling that it might not be too long before our family grows again, at least not if my daughter's expression is to be believed. That I have a new grandson, even if he isn't my own blood, means that I should be grateful for what I have, and in that, I have my daughter back, safely, and a new son who seems to be willing to humor me. There are times I probably wouldn't have realized how lucky I am with that. But I have learned, over the years."

Telin laughed from where he stood, "You have more grace with this than you did with almost any of the others. Not only was it hard to get you to agree to Kelu's marrying Uhbara, but it was difficult getting your acceptance of any of Hlasa or Seenah or Syal. Maybe this time we'll get things started right."

Hela looked down, then leaned forward to kiss her father on his cheek. "Thank you, Father. This is going to cause interesting problems, but I'm glad you're being reasonable."

He laughed, gesturing to his brother, "If you need to thank anyone for that, you should thank him, since I learned long ago not to argue with him. But I'm grateful that this is formal, if only because we don't need anyone with a reputation like my brother's was."

Uncle Telin laughed, "I think I was outdone by our nephew. Another daughter was introduced before I left with these two in tow. Hopefully that's all of them. But Redel's loyalty to Ael'yn is as solid as mine to Selah. We've both gone beyond our mistakes, and it seems that these two might have too. But, I should get them back where they can rest. Hela, if you have anything left here, you should get it, because you'll want it at your new home." His words made everything seem better, and Hela ran off into the room that she shared with Miana while she was in town. It wouldn't be hers any longer, but it was well done. She was going home now, to a new husband and son. Life had changed, but perhaps for the better.

www.ingramcontent.com/pod-product-compliance
Lightning Source LLC
LaVergne TN
LVHW012050160826
845678LV00014B/2771

* 9 7 9 8 8 4 7 9 9 6 5 9 4 *